Sir Charles Alfred Elliott

Laborious days : leaves from the Indian record of Sir Charles Alfred Elliott

Sir Charles Alfred Elliott

Laborious days : leaves from the Indian record of Sir Charles Alfred Elliott

ISBN/EAN: 9783337305604

Printed in Europe, USA, Canada, Australia, Japan

Cover: Foto ©Andreas Hilbeck / pixelio.de

More available books at **www.hansebooks.com**

LABORIOUS DAYS.

LEAVES FROM THE INDIAN RECORD

OF

SIR CHARLES ALFRED ELLIOTT,

K.C.S.I., C.I.E., &C., &C.,

LIEUTENANT-GOVERNOR OF BENGAL.

———◆———

CALCUTTA:

PRINTED BY J. LARKINS,

AT THE PERSEVERANCE PRINTING WORKS, 132, LOWER CIRCULAR ROAD.

———

1892.

TO

LADY ELLIOTT,

WHOSE GENTLE INFLUENCE BRIGHTENS HER HUSBAND'S HOME

, AND LESSENS THE BURDEN OF HIS OFFICIAL CARES,

THIS LITTLE SKETCH OF HIS BRILLIANT CAREER

IS RESPECTFULLY DEDICATED

BY

THE AUTHOR.

PREFACE.

ONE of the most promising signs of the times we live in is the preference shown by the reading public for memoirs and records of discovery and travel. The new bias is a reaction from the love of fiction which characterized the last generation. It, indeed, was fortunate in possessing such literary giants as Dickens and Thackeray, not to mention minor stars in the galaxy of genius which illustrated the early Victorian era. The taste created by the immortal Waverley Novels, and kept alive by successors not unworthy to occupy the throne of the Wizard of the North, is now catered for by authors of a very different calibre. We have been pelted with romances in thousands, until every passion has been torn to tatters and the changes rung on every possible incident of human life. Those who are familiar with the under-currents which influence public opinion have long since been aware that the reign of the novelist is hastening to decay. The fact is not to be regretted; for fiction, save of the very first quality, tends to dilute the sympathies and impair the judgment.

The rise of biography in public esteem is especially a matter for congratulation. There 'is no greater spur to exertion than the exploits of our fellows. What man has done, we reflect, man can do. I venture to think that the life-story told in this little book will not be without its effect on the formation of character. I claim not the skill of a Plutarch, whose enthralling pages have led many a youth to emulate the noble deeds which they embalm. Nor does my subject lend itself to such treatment. Sir Charles Elliott, at the outset of his Indian career, looked face to face at war in its direst form : but for more than a third of a century his lines have 'been cast, if not always in pleasant, at least in peaceful places, and his victories have been those of civil life. Had he fallen on times of civil stress, there can be little doubt that his indomitable energy and power of impressing his personality upon others would have placed him in the first rank as a man of action. But the great value of his life is the lesson it affords *nil sine labore*; freely translated by Macaulay as " Genius consists in a capacity for taking pains." This is, indeed, a truism : but it is constantly forgotten in these fevered times of ours, when men mistake notoriety for distinction and struggle to rise by self-advertisement and by picking the brains of others.

The plan of this work has precluded my adding those touches so welcome to the gentle reader which lift the veil of private life and exhibit the subject of a biography in his relations with friends, family and dependents. It has been said truly that to know a man one must see him at home. Sir Charles Elliott's character would lose nothing by such a scrutiny. In the brief intervals of relaxation from duties which would crush an ordinary man, he appears in an amiable light—a warm-hearted friend, devoted to family ties, and one whose culture has not outgrown his sense of humour. While glorying in his work and investing its dryest details with a halo of enthusiasm he enjoys with equal zest the active pleasures that life affords. He is still an ardent pedestrian, oarsman and mountaineer; and, in his younger days, he was an excellent shot. The Miltonian quotation from which I have borrowed my title by no means applies to him in its entirety.

My acknowledgments are due to Babu Kally Prosonno Dey, Editor of the *National Magazine*, for permission to reprint the chapters of this little work which originally appeared in that interesting periodical.

To Rai Bahádur Jaiprakás Lál, C.I.E., Diwan of the Dumraon Ráj, I am indebted for a subscription covering the cost of a sufficient number of copies of this book to guarantee me against pecuniary loss. This is a great matter in a land where the success of literary ventures is so uncertain. Profit I do not desire. I write in the interests of truth and justice; and it will suffice for me if a perusal of this little work should correct mistaken estimates of Sir Charles Elliott's public character, and lead to a wider recognition of the great services he has rendered to the Government and people of this country.

CHAPTER I.

HISTORY OF UNAO.

———◆———

Because it is an ability not common to write a good history, as
may well appear by the small number of them ; yet if
particularity of actions memorable were but liberally re-
ported, the compiling of a complete history of the times
might be the better expected when a writer should arise
that were fit for it : for the collection of such relations
might be as a nursery garden, whereby to plant a fair and
stately garden when time should serve.

BACON'S ADVANCEMENT OF LEARNING.

IT is a staple complaint with educated Indians
that Englishmen are unsympathetic. Permeated
as many are with western culture, and conscious of
moral and intellectual affinities with the ruling
race, they resent the apparent want of interest in
themselves and their aspirations exhibited by the
Anglo-Indian community at large. They point to
the giants of a past age—the generation of Sir
William Jones—and the galaxy of bright visitants
whose love for the land of their sojourn was only
equalled by their craving desire to explore the
secret recesses of her history, laws and religion.
The contrast between past and present in this respect is, indeed, discouraging ; and not less so the
growing divergence between forces which united
might revolutionize Asiatic society within the

life-time of a generation. Those, however, who
are inclined to impute all the blame to English insularity and racial pride would do well to
ask themselves whether other and less obvious
causes are not at work. The proximity of Europe,
with its ever-widening scope for mental and physical enjoyment, renders the comparative stagnation of India more intolerable than it could have
been to the eighteenth century Englishman. He
was never confronted by demands from subject
races for social and political equality, and played
unquestioned the grateful part of patron. Our
best and brightest intellects of to-day are too
often benumbed by a crushing routine and im-
paired by the irritation arising from a sense of
injustice. Often, too, they dwindle under the
atrophy encountered in our Hill-resorts with an
atmosphere of officialism and soul-less frivolity.
Hence the undoubted fact that, with all her material progress, Imperial India can boast of no
single contribution to that which De Quincey terms
the Literature of Power. Thoughtful men of
every race will agree that the time has come for
a united effort to remove this reproach. Good
government, improved facilities for locomotion,
and the interchange of ideas are but a means to
an end—the elevation of humanity. Those who
keep that great object in view will take the fullest
advantage of the mechanism afforded by modern

science : but they will soar high above the world of the engineer, the organizer, and the soldier. They will devote their best energies to "the proper study of mankind "—not in view of gratifying an idle curiosity or adding a zest to lettered ease, but that they may be able to gauge the defects of society and suggest remedies for the countless ills against which religion and science alike have hitherto striven in vain. Now human society is incarnate history : and he who wishes to grasp its real import and tendencies must compel the past to yield its varied stores. A rich and almost untrodden field lies open to such a man. Our official records, in spite of the ravages of Philistinism,* are a mine of wealth to the explorer. The archives of our great families teem with curious lore which is gladly placed at the disposal of the judicious enquirer. Lastly, the people still possess a vast wealth of tradition and floating legend which awaits its Grimm or its Niebuhr to yield results of priceless value to the student of sociology. So bewildering, indeed, is the mass of material at hand that the would-be historian knows not where to begin, and dreads the dissipation of his energies

---

* A collector of Murshidabad some years back, wishing to write a history of that little-known period which separates the acquisition of the Diwanny from the reforms of Cornwallis, was deterred by the discovery of a gap of fifteen years in his records ! A predecessor had burned several tons of priceless papers relating to the years 1772—1787 in order to find room for current ones,

on a task which may launch him on a boundless ocean of research. But let such a one take heart of grace. He will find in any British district a compact and manageable unit: and the industry of many working in parallel channels will soon afford a vast mass of data for generalization and synthesis. The author ventures to think that, by laying before his readers the very pith and marrow of a district history which is a model of its kind, he may tempt some of them to follow his example, and perhaps to deserve equally well of posterity.

Unao, we learn from *Hunter's Gazetteer*, is a district of the Lucknow Division of the North-Western Provinces, embracing 1,747 square miles of the vast alluvial plain traversed by the sacred Ganges. The census population in 1881 was rather less than 900,000: all engaged in tilling the fertile loam whose crop-bearing power is enhanced by assiduous irrigation. Devoid of interesting features, with no centres of learning, industry or the arts, a more unpromising field for historical research can hardly be conceived than is afforded by this little nineteenth century Bœotia. But enthusiasm sustained by dogged resolution makes light of obstacles: and thirty years ago Unao was fortunate enough to possess a chief who was endowed with these qualities in a marked degree. In 1860 the present Lieutenant-Governor of Bengal,

then Mr. Charles Alfred Elliott, found himself
Deputy Commissioner of Unao, and straightway
resolved to preserve its history and tradition from
unmerited oblivion.   His education fitted him ad-
mirably for the self-appointed task.   Born twenty-
five years previously, he had enjoyed the priceless
boon of a public school and University training.
He was, indeed, a scholar on the great foundation
of Trinity College, Cambridge, when the seduc-
tions of an Indian career proved too strong for
the aspirations which he may well have cherished
of acquiring academic distinction.   In June 1856
he passed the second open Examination for our
Civil Service, and came out to this country in the
November of that year.   While he was still a
student at Benares, the mutiny whirlwind swept over
the land and gave him opportunities of gaining experience and distinction which young civilians of
these humdrum days may sigh for in vain.   He
embraced them with ardour, was attached to General Franks' forces on the borders of Oudh, and
afterwards to those of Sir Hope Grant and General Kelly; and was twice mentioned in despatches.
The restoration of the British peace found him
ready and willing to exchange the sword for the
pen.   After spells of service as Assistant Commissioner of Faizabad and Civil Judge and Town
Magistrate of Lucknow, he became Officiating
Deputy Commissioner of Unao at an age when

modern civilians deem themselves fortunate ἰἰ they
are entrusted with the destinies of a sub-division.
The spirit in which Mr. Elliott began his labours
as annalist of Unao shines through the preface of
his admirable little history, which was printed for
private circulation in 1861. He tells us that he
wished to put to a crucial test his belief that the
history of an average district would be of value
to local officials and residents, to the student and
the general reader. He laments the absence of
works of a similar scope—a fact due to ignorance
of the results derivable from careful investigation
and an unjustly low estimate of the value of col-
lated tradition. His remarks on this head are
singularly far-seeing in so young an author, and
richly merit quotation. "Like all half-educated
races," he writes, "the Hindus place an inordinate
value on their mythical and historical traditions,
and are greatly pleased to find an Englishman in
an official position enquiring into them ; while the
reputation of being acquainted with out-of-the-
way facts, not ascertainable in the ordinary official
routine, creates in their minds a presumption of
general information as to the state of the district,
and makes them more communicative on matters
respecting which a private enquiry is often necessary. Thus a knowledge of the popular traditions
and ballads gives to the possessor an influence
over the people and the key to their hearts. Even

if this book were of no further use than as a record to be kept in the Unao office, I should still
feel a pleasure in presenting it, for the benefit of
future officials, as a small return to the district
for the pleasant memories with which it is associated in my mind, and as a testimony of the
interest I felt in it and of the esteem and regard in
which I hold some of its taluqdars and residents.
The common disregard of tradition as a vehicle
for historical truth springs, I think, from two
causes—from our general distrust of native accuracy, and from the exposure by Niebuhr and Sir
George C. Lewis of the fallacy of the traditional
basis on which the history of Rome as it used to
be written rested. But it is one thing to rely on
a single tradition, such as Livy's, composed evidently in the interest of certain families, and dead
and stereotyped long ago, and quite another thing
to question a multitude of living, conflicting traditions, and after testing and trying them in every
way by comparison with each other and with external landmarks, to collect from the alembic of
close enquiry a precipitate of historical fact.
None of the objections urged against the validity
of tradition in Niebuhr's famous chapter apply to
such a treatment of it as this native inaccuracy
tends all in one direction—to the glorification of
the subject of the story; and thus the error being
constant it can be eliminated in a general enquiry.

Where a story praises A above B, and B sets B above A, the mutual self-glorification neutralizes itself."

Thus the keynote to our author's treatment of tradition is to be found in a pregnant remark of a predecessor in the same line of research, that *concurrence between isolated traditions is almost equivalent to authentic history.* He compares versions current among different clans as well as those told in different families of the same class, and reads them by the light of general history. This process of sublimation gives a residuum of fairly trustworthy narrative, illustrating events often of great importance in their bearing on the formation of a people's character and the development of their civilization. Tradition apart, a mass of documentary evidence had to be dealt with. This included sunnuds, safe guides as regards facts and dates; family records, only worthy of evidence when they concern contemporary events; and certain *obiter dicta* in a Persian school book then in great request. From these somewhat unpromising materials Mr. Elliott contrived to extract a mass of information enabling his readers to trace the history of Unao from the earliest days. We see the little district in the mythical era a portion of classic Ajodhya, the realm of good king Dasarath, and the chosen above of saints and warriors. Anon the curtain lifts and gives us a glimpse of a land clothed with dense forests, the habitat of wild aboriginal tribes. These give way before the invasion of the fair-skinned Aryan, and take refuge in the hill region northward, whence, about the commencement of the Christian era, they swoop down on their conquerors and drive them even unto distant Guzerat. Twelve hundred years later we view an immigration of chivalrous Rajputs driven from the centres of Hindu power and devotion by the fierce Shahabuddin Gori. A century later the followers of the Prophet pour in and establish colonies throughout the land, which pave the way for its assimilation with the Empire of Akbar. The reign of the Mogul is graphically portrayed, with its elaborate fiscal system, its centralization tempered by checks and counter checks. Then we see how, when paralysis strikes the heart of the effete organization, satraps throw off their allegiance; and one of them bribes the English successors of his master to recognize him as sovereign of Oudh. The description which follows of the *Nawabi* rule, its lawlessness and elasticity as contrasted, not altogether unfavourably, with the inexorable justice that followed the annexation, enables us to understand why the very excellences of the British regime prompted the whole population of Oudh to range themselves on the national side in the crisis of the Mutiny.

But Government is, after all, less a question of laws than of the personal character of those appointed to administer them. Our author's peroration is a passage of equal eloquence and truth, and deserves to be written in letters of gold in every Secretariat of the Empire. " The Native of India," he writes, " has no valet mind : he can worship the true hero when he knows him. And as long as the British Government can send such men as Major Henry Evans* to govern its districts, to walk uprightly in its service, and to lead its subjects up through education and a love of law to religion and a love of God, so long will the future of Unao be bright indeed."

He who desires to be well acquainted with a people will not reject their popular stories and superstitions. These are the words of Sir John Malcolm, a past master of statecraft, for whom the oriental mind had no secrets. His dictum applies with twofold force to the historian of an Indian community : for in no part of the globe have these legends, which pitiless science terms myths, exercised a profounder influence on the formation of national character. History proverbially repeats itself : and the key to many a complex problem of life and action is afforded by a minute study of those glorious epics which are among the

---

* The first Deputy Commissioner of Unao.

most precious inheritances of the Aryan Race.
Here the ancient altars stand decked with greener
bays than those of Greece and Rome in colder
climes. The Ramayana, Mahabharata, and Purans,
with their pictures of virile bravery and womanly
self-devotion, still live in the hearts of millions
and insensibly influence their daily lives. Their
very blots and blemishes, the blurred outlines
which reveal their hoary antiquity are cherished
with a loving care; and episodes, which to the
matter-of-fact European are but the stuff that
dreams are made of, are vivid realities in the eyes
of the faithful Hindu.   Sir Charles Elliott has,
therefore, done wisely to devote a chapter of his
history to the mythical age of Unao: albeit that
most of the legends current in the district are but
variants charged with local colouring of stories
found in epic poesy. That of Lona Chamarin
merits quotation in our author's own graphic words,
if only for the proof it affords that Hindu methods
of culture have remained the same for countless
ages.   Lona was a woman of the despised caste
of leather-dressers, and lived at Unao.   One day,
while bathing in the Ganges, she found a caldron
full of flesh which had been cast ashore near the
temple of Puriur.   This was the mortal spoils of
Dhanattar Vaid, who had been killed by the snake,
typifying in mythology the Scythian invasion of
India, lest by his cunning he should save king

Parichit from a similar fate. Lona ate the flesh :
and as she ate, the wisdom of Dhanattar passed
into her. She became skilful in cures and medi-
cines, and if any was bitten by a snake she healed
him. There came a day when all the people of
Unao were transplanting the young rice-plants
from their seed-beds to the wider fields in which
they were to grow. Every man brought the plants
in a basket and threw them out in one place where
Lona was standing : but when they came back
with another basketful they found that she had
planted out all the plants which were in the heap.
When they saw this they wondered greatly, and
said, "We are two hundred men bringing baskets
of plants, how can one woman plant out so many
all alone ? " So, at last, when the rest went away
after emptying their baskets, her brother-in-law
stayed behind and hid himself. He watched and
saw that when all were gone Lona stripped herself
naked and took up the heap in her hands, and
muttered words, and cast the plants into the air,
and all the rice-plants planted themselves out in
order, each in its proper line and place. Then he
cried out in astonishment, and when she saw
that she was watched, she was overpowered with
shame, and crouching down tried to escape. Her
brother-in-law followed to reassure her, but she
fled the faster, and as she fled the earth opened
before her, and behind her all the water from the

rice-fields, collecting in one wave, flowed down the channel which she made. At first she crouched as she ran, but when she saw she was pursued she rose up, and the channel became deeper, and the wave behind her rose higher, and fear added wings to her flight. So she sped along, carrying destruction through the country as she ran; passing through the town of Newayan until she reached the Ganges at Dalarmau and rushed into it and hid her shame in its water. The channel which she made is called the Lona Naddi to this day. The flood destroyed the town of Newayan, and left nothing but a high mound which stands close to the bank of the stream. Sir Charles Elliott adds a foot-note to the effect that *mantras* for charming away the evil effects of snake-bite are still addressed to Lona Chamarin: but they are not popular, for any one knowing them is bound to go to the assistance of the victim who pronounces them: a necessity which might sometimes prove inconvenient to the onlooker. Those who have lived in the little island of Jersey will remember that ancient formula the *Clameur de Haro,* an appeal to a long-defunct Duke of Normandy famed for strong administration and justice, which, uttered by any one whose rights are invaded at once suspends all proceedings to his detriment.

As materials for history, however, the value of myths is nought and the annals of Unao are a

blank till its conquest by the Mahommedans in
the thirteenth century of our era. At that date
the Unao Pargana was tenanted by a colony of
Bisseins from Gorakhpur, whose king Anwanta is
supposed to have given his name to the district.
Further west there was a large settlement of
Chandels, driven from Chanderi in the Deccan by
the Chohan victorious in that great battle which is
best described in the terms of a proverb used in
cases where might conquers right—*Khet Pri-*
thora, talwar Ala aur Udal ka. " The victory
was Prithi-Raj's, but the glory lay with Ala and
Udal." The present pargana of Bangarmau was
the seat of the Rajpuri clan, the chief of which
was a tributary of the kingdom of Kanouj. Its
capital was at Rajkot, where to this day vast ruins
extend over an area of several miles. The streams
which wash the base of mounds a hundred feet high
lay bare cyclopic masonry and sometimes gold
coin and jewellery stamped with quaint legends
which bring disaster on their finders. A Brahmin
community was found at Safipur : and a cluster of
low-caste herdsmen in the central portion of the
district. In the east lived the Bhars, an aboriginal race, which at one time dominated the eastern
half of Oudh. Their earliest habitat was Bahraich,
which is said to owe its name to them : and they
have left indelible traces on the nomenclature of
the upper Gangetic delta.

When we approach the Mahommedan conquest we stand on firmer ground. In the year 1193
A.D., writes Sir Charles Elliott, Shahabuddin Ghori
conquered and slew the hero of Rajput chronicles,
Raja Prithora of Delhi: and in the next year
he overthrew his great rival, Raja Jaichand of
Canouj. These important victories were followed
up by vigorous attacks in all directions. The
sacred Mount Abu, the impenetrable Gwalior, the
holy Benares, Gya and Ajmir and Anhalwara
Patan—all the great centres of Rajput power and
Hindu devotion—were startled by the appearance
before their walls of the uncouth barbarians. All,
after a brave but vain resistance, fell before his
sword. The Brahmin folded his hands and cursed
the *Mleccha,* but not openly. The merchant
sought to turn an honest penny by him, and was
oftener paid with iron than with gold. The Sudra
served the strange highlanders much as he had
obeyed his Aryan master. But to the Rajput this
upsetting of his received ideas was intolerable.
It was part of his religion that his race should
be lords of the lands; and to see his Raja bow
before a barbarian was desecration and impiety.
By mutual jealousies, by incapacity for combination, and by fatuous negligence, the country had
been taken from him, and the lives of his great
Rajas had been lost. Now at last, thoroughly
roused when it was too late, he felt that it was

impossible to remain quiet under defeat. If he could not fight he could fly; some spot might be found where, though only for a little space, he might be beyond the conqueror's reach. The outcome of this great movement was the colonization of Unao by warlike Rajput clans. Another class of these settlers owe their origin to grants of land bestowed on their ancestors by Mogul emperors for services in war. Under Akbar's liberal sway Rajputs were prized as the very flower of the army. Alliances with princesses of their stock were eagerly sought for by the Mahommedan nobility—nay, by the imperial family, itself. Both Jehangir and Shah Jehan were Rajputs on the mother's side. These colonies reproduced all the essential features of European feudality. The tract occupied by the settlers was held under a special grant from the king. The grantee was bound to do service in the field against rebels or disturbers of the peace when called on by the proper authorities: and sometimes it was stipulated that he should attend the Faujdar on his excursions through the country with a fixed force. Sixteen great clans of Rajputs still survive in Unao, each with its own well-defined tract of country. The royal house of Bulrampur is an offshoot of one of these,—the Junwars, found in the Bangarmau Pargana. From another branch was descended the infamous Jussa Singh who

during the Mutiny seized the English fugitives
escaping by boat from Futtehgurh and delivered
them to the ruthless Nana, by whose orders they
were done to death on the Cawnpore parade-ground.
The Dikhits are a second important Rajput class;
asserting a lineal descent from the children of the
Sun who ruled Ajodhya for fifty-one generations.
Though still in possession of a large and compact
area in Unao, they are but a shadow of their
former selves. Their downfall dates from the
opposition offered by their Raja Prithimal to the
assimilation of Oudh by the Emperor Akbar.
When the Vizier of Mahommad Shah Adili, says
Sir Charles Elliott, led his forces to oppose the
return of Humayun, all Hindustan was moved to
see a Hindu once more at the head of affairs and
combating a Mahommedan in the field, and a vast
army flocked to his standard. This feeling gave
to the campaign something of the nature of a
religious war; and, as a natural result, the victory
of Akbar spread over all the country the fear of
a forcible conversion to Islamism. This fear was
probably the immediate cause which prevented
Prithimal from obeying the summons of Akbar's
general, Mahommad Amin Khan, who was appointed to the government of Oudh. Though
treated with the greatest courtesy, and repeatedly
called on to submit, he refused to return any
answer whatever to the summons, but sent his

B

four Ranis to their fathers' homes, and called a
council of feudatories and followers to discuss the
conduct of the war. . . . Some counselled him
to meet the enemy in the field, and others warn-
ed him to keep within the ramparts of his fort:
but not one spoke of surrender. Meanwhile the
Delhi force had crossed the Ganges by a bridge
of boats below Canouj, and encamped before the
fort of Patheora. Then was seen the resolution
which the council of war had decided on. Clad
in full armour, and followed by all his captains
dressed in their saffron robes, the Raja issued
into the plain and drew up his forces for the
battle. The Moghal yoked his guns together to
withstand their impetuous charge; but twice his
staunchest battalions were driven back and twice
a shameful rout was imminent, when fresh reserves
came up. But the unequal contest was now all
but over. Bhagiruth Singh, the Chohan, had already fallen: other chiefs were wounded, and the
Rajputs were weary and dispirited. Then the
Moghal cavalry were brought up fresh to the
attack. Latta Singh Chandel headed one desperate charge and fell drowned, as the bard phras-
es it, in that sea of horsemen. The enemy swept
on in one irresistible wave over Prithimal and his
captains, who fell each in their places, and the
power of the Dikhits was for ever broken. The
Chohans formed another tide of Rajput immigra-

tion. Their advent was, according to tradition, due to an old man's uxoriousness. A Chohan Raja of Mainpuri, the hereditary chief of all Rajputs beyond Rajasthan, married again late in life, though his former wife had borne him two sons. The bride was averse to be an old man's darling, and stipulated that, if she bore a son, he should succeed to the family possessions. The Raja eagerly closed with these hard terms, but did not long survive his bliss. A posthumous son was born, and the young Rani produced her deed and claimed its execution. The injustice was patent, but there was no help for it. Rajput honour demanded that the contract should be strictly enforced. The slighted elder brother left their patrimony in disgust and settled in Unao.

The second great class of Rajput emigrants—those in the enjoyment of jaghirs for military service—includes the clans of Sengor and Gaur. Sir Charles Elliott gives an episode in the history of the former which places the lawlessness of Nawabi rule in a startling light. Umrao Singh, an eight-anna shareholder in the village of Kantha, was sold up in 1848 for default in paying revenue. Like other desperate men in those days he took to the road, and, joining another bandit named Baljor Singh of Parsandan, was the prime mover in many a dacoity. In 1850 this precious pair at the head of five hundred followers had the

hardihood to attack the king's Chackladaí, who
was encamped at Bainsora with a loyal Sengor
chief named Runjit Singh, a thousand troops, and
two cannon.   But the royal artillery had only two
rounds per gun ; and after discharging their pieces
they incontinently fled.   Deprived of their moral
support, the rest of the Chackladar's army followed
suit, and the rebels looted the royal camp and
dragged off the guns in triumph.   It was, however, short-lived.   The outraged Chackladar returned with stronger forces and abundant ammunition,
and carried fire and sword into every village which
had opposed him.   It is only what might have
been expected to find Baljor and Umrao promi-
nent in the rebel ranks during the Mutiny ; while
Ranjit Singh was equally active on the English
side.   The Gaurs are settled in Tuppeh Bunthur,
which was traditionally occupied in Akbar's reign
by a race of cowherds who paid an annual tribute
of ghee to government.   Actuated either by in-
solence or knavery—two characteristics not unknown in the Goalas of our own time—the Gaddis,
as they were called, filled the earthen vessels in
which the tribute was sent with cowdung and
covered it with a thin layer of ghee.   On the
discovery of their fraud at Delhi, a Gaur who held
a high military command was told off to punish
the insubordinate ones.   He carried out the royal
behest by exterminating them and annexing their

territory. Kesri Singh, a later chief of Bunthur,
came into collision with a tribe of Chandels in
occupation of another Tuppeh of Harha on a
boundary question. The reign of law had not
begun, and there was no other resource but an
appeal to arms. A sanguinary encounter took
place regulated by the code of Rajput chivalry.
Man after man on either side came to the front
and challenged a foe to single combat. Thus
the whole of the forces was speedily engaged, and
the slaughter was as great as that under similar
conditions recorded in Walter Scott's *Fair Maid
of Perth*. The Chandel leader wounded Kesri
Singh so desperately that he could not stir from
the spot where he fell ; and as quarter was neither
asked nor given in those good old times, he would
infallibly have been slaughtered had not a merciful Brahmin surreptitiously dragged him unto a
bed of dry rushes. Here he was sought by his
blood-thirsty foes, who thought of setting the
rushes on fire as the simplest method of destroy-
ing him. But the Brahmin again saved Kesri's
life by swearing that the field was his, and that
the sale of rush baskets was his only means of
livelihood. Seeing them incredulous, he proceeded to assure them that if they fired the rushes he
would cut his throat there and then, and a Brahmin's blood would be on their guilty heads. This
awful threat was sufficient. The Chandels with-

drew. Kesri was carried to the Brahmin's hut where he soon recovered to take the field again and turn the tables on his enemies.

Sir Charles Elliott's chapter on the Rajput colonization of Unao ends with the story of the great Bais clan, who, though not strictly speaking settlers in that district, claimed a lordship over seven of its parganas. As is customary with Rajputs, the Bais assert a miraculous descent. Their ancestor was none other than Salavahana, the son of a mighty serpent who conquered king Vikramajit of Ujani and exercised the unique privilege of fixing his own era which begins A.D. 55. There is, however, a hiatus of twelve centuries in their annals; and we do not hear of them again till 1250, when two scions of the tribe named Abhai Chand and Nirbhai Chand won glory by rescuing the Queen of the Gautam Raja of Angul from the clutches of the Mahommedan governor of Oudh. The Raja had omitted the formality of paying tribute, and the Governor in revenge despatched a strong force to intercept the Rani while on a pilgrimage to Buxar for the purpose of bathing in the Ganges. The Rajput brothers happened to be passing when the helpless lady's palanquin was attacked; and, moved by her piteous appeals for help against the barbarians, they charged the assailants and drove them off. Nirbhai Chand fell a victim to his valour, but Abhai Chand survived to wed the daughter and heiress of the grateful Raja, and to succeed with the title of Rao to all the Gautam possessions north of the Ganges. Tilak Chand, the seventh in descent from the hero of this romantic story, is a name still familiar to Baises throughout Oudh. He flourished in the fifteenth century, and extended the empire of his clan over twenty-two parganas. Tilak Chand was the premier Raja of Oudh, and innumerable legends of his power and prowess are sung by local bards. Two clans are found to this day in Unao who are Rajputs by courtesy, though not by blood, because the great Rao brought them within the sacred pale. The Mahrors were originally low-born Kahars who carried Tilak Chand out of an action fought with the Pathans of Mulhiabad. It was the only defeat of his glorious career. A panic seized his troops, who deserted their chief wounded in his litter; but his faithful bearers stood by him and beat off the foe. The Rao afterwards declared that his Rajputs on that day were women and his Kahars Rajputs: and then the poor Mehras (palki-bearers) became Mahrors and gave their daughters in marriage to Rajputs of blue blood. The Rawats are another class of " Tilak Chandi Rajputs," and boast an illegitimate descent from the great epony-mous hero of the Bais. Mitrajit, the seventh Rao from Tilak Chand, is second only to him in the estimation of the clansmen. Sir Charles Elliott tells us that when Mitrajit first went to Delhi, he attended the Durbar, but stood outside the entrance expecting some one to invite him in. He waited till it was all over, and when the Rajas of Jaipur and Marwar were passing out, they noticed his uncouth country air and manners, and asked who he was. They were told " a Raja of Baiswara." One asked why he wore two swords. " To fight any two men who dare to meet me " was the proud reply. The others asked why he did not enter the Durbar but stood without the door. He replied that in his country it was customary to invite the stranger, and not leave him to push his way in uninvited. However, he said, as *they* had given their daughters and sisters to the king, they would not be looked on as strangers and had a perfect right to enter. Incensed at this insult they challenged him to single combat. Mitrajit came to the field mounted on a mare, which, at the first onset, became unmanageable and bolted with him. He pulled her up with great trouble, and dismounted, pronouncing a curse on any member of his race who should in future bestride a mare. He then returned to the field on foot and discomfited both his foes. To this day no Bais of his house can be induced to mount a mare. Mitrajit's exploit took wind, and he rose to high favour in the Imperial Court. He was entrusted with the command of an army sent to Cabul, where in a dangerous mountain pass he met and defeated the enemy. Elated by the victory, he ordered his kettledrum to sound the note of triumph, but their hoarse booming brought down an avalanche of snow which buried the greater portion of his host. Thus he fell into disgrace at Delhi and returned to his home a broken man. It is not a little curious that a tradition such as this should survive for centuries and be repeated by thousands who have never seen snow and can form no conception of its nature and appearance.

Sir Charles Elliott repeats one more tale of Rajput prowess, which is interesting by reason of the light it throws on the rough and ready methods employed by the native government of old time in the collection of revenue. When Sa'adat Khan, the founder of the royal house of Oudh, became provincial governor in 1723, he found the revenue administration in the direst disorder : and just as Warren Hastings did half a century later, he made a progress through the country in order to see things with his own eyes. When he reached a place called Morawan in Baiswara, he summoned the canungos and ordered them to produce the *dauls* or rent-rolls of their respective parganas. They asked what daul his Highness wanted, explaining that there were two— the " coward's daul " and the " man's daul." In the first, the zemindar was charged only with the sum fixed at the previous settlement, but 'in the second his rent was raised in proportion to inter- mediate improvements. The Subadar called for the " man's daul," and doubled the assessment of Baiswara with a stroke of his pen.   Then he summoned the agents of all the Rajas to a Dur- bar, where he sat with a heap of *pan* leaves on one side and a heap of bullets on the other. Addressing the crowd, he bade them, if their masters accepted his terms, to take up the *pan* leaves : if not the bullets.   One by one they step- ped forward and humbly took up a *pan* leaf each. Sa'adat Khan turned to his courtiers and said with a sneer—" I had heard great things of the fighting men of Baiswara, but they seem readier to pay than to fight."   But he was premature in his judgment.   The agent of Cheitrai, an illegiti- mate member of the clan, stood last in Durbar by reason of his master's bar sinister.   When his turn came, he said " Nawab, my master was ready to accept your terms ; but if you wish to see now a Bais can fight he will not refuse to gratify you. Give him but a day to prepare himself, and then lead your forces against his fort."   Sa'adat Khan agreed, and attacked Cheitrai's stronghold on the morrow.   But he found it a hard nut to crack. All day long the battle raged, and the besiegers were baffled.   In the evening the Nawab sent to say that he was quite satisfied with the specimen he had afforded of Baiswara prowess, and that he would let Cheitrai off with half the assessment fixed in his case. The terms were accepted and Cheitrai rose high in the esteem of government.

The Mutiny divided Rajputs in Unao. The vast majority joined the national side, for the hostility to British rule throughout Oudh was indescribably bitter.* Some, however, defied public opinion and met with a rich reward. Amongst the loyal few were the Magarwara Rajputs, who lived but five miles from Cawnpore on the Lucknow road. In spite of their proximity to the great rebel centre, these people assisted the English army with information and supplies, and accompanied Sir Henry Havelock in his ineffectual advance on Unao and Basiratganj. When he retreated to Cawnpore they left their homes and followed him ; nor did they leave his standard when they saw their village in flames—destroyed

---

* The cause of this hostility was, in some measure, the national pride of the people of Oudh. Thirty years before the annexation, Bishop Heber, while on his progress up-country, met a Captain Lockitt at Lucknow, who told him that he had recently had a conversation with an old jemadar of cavalry, who spoke out like the rest of his countrymen on the weakness of the king and the wickedness of the Government. Captain Lockitt asked the old man how he would like being placed under the British Government. " Miserable as we are," he exclaimed, of all miseries " keep us from that ! " " Why so ? " asked Captain Lockitt. " Are not our people better governed ? " Yes, was the answer : " but the name of Oudh and the honor of our nation would be at an end."

by the rebels as a warning to sympathizers with the Feringhis.

We have seen an indirect result of the Mahommedan conquest of India in the settlement of Rajput colonies throughout Oudh. It remains to consider the effect on the popular character produced by the introduction of a fresh strain of blood, and on social history by new ideas and a new administrative policy. The first wave of invasion rolled in from Ghazni, whence Masud, the fiery nephew of Sultan Mahmud, set forth in 1030 A.D. to plant the green flag of Islam in places which had never yet re-echoed praises of God the Highest, the most Merciful. He took Delhi and was welcomed at Canouj. But when he crossed the Ganges and penetrated further into Oudh, he was stoutly opposed by a confederacy of powerful Rajas who drove him into Bahraich and cut his army in pieces. Three hundred years elapsed ere any Mahommedan obtained a foot-hold in Oudh. Between the 14th and 17th centuries their colonies slowly increased, but they have long been stationary, and at the present day the Hindus are more than 93 per cent. of the population. The early conquests were the outcome of blood-feuds or other forms of private revenge ; and the struggle between the creeds had none of the features of a religious war. There is, indeed, a strong tendency among the

followers of the Prophet to assimilate in all ex-
ternals with their Hindu neighbours. In the
matter of diet they are as scrupulous as any
Brahmin. The *dhuti* is commonly worn by
them, and the formula *Ram Ram* their ordinary
mode of salutation. In short, the law which
ordains that the greater body shall attract the less
is, or was till lately, in as full operation in Unao
as it was in Eastern Bengal before the great neo-
puritan revival which is stirring Islam to its
depths had placed an impassable gulf between
the professors of the rival creeds. Bangarmau,
so often mentioned in these annals, was the
theatre of the first Mahommedan effort at colonization. According to tradition, about the year
1300 A.D. a saint named Alauddin came from
Canouj with the intention of living peaceably in
the territories of Raja Nala of Newal. But the
Raja would not tolerate the presence of a *mleccha,*
and endeavoured to eject him. The holy man
cursed his persecutor; and straightway the city
of Newal turned upside down, burying its inhabitants. Utensils of archaic form are to this day
exposed by the plough amongst the extensive
ruins of king Newal's luckless city; and those
who stand upon ancient ways see a confirmation
of the legend in the fact that they are always
found inverted. The catastrophe was probably
due to an earthquake in prehistoric times. After

this exhibition of superhuman power Alauddin
founded the town of Bangamau, which still contains a leaven of Shaikh and Sayyid families.
The more important settlement at Sufipur, or
Saipur, dates from 1431, when Ibrahim Shah of
Jaunpur, to revenge the insult offered to another
saint known as Maulana Shaha Ikram by the
refusal of five Rajas to allow him to sound the
azam, or summons to prayers, marched a strong
force into their territory and defeated them with
great slaughter. The victory cost one of the
Musulman generals his life. His grave, which is
still pointed out at Sufipur, has rare and precious
virtues in a country which suffers greatly from
droughts. In the event of one occurring, all that
is necessary is to milk a cow and mix the milk
with ten maunds of flour, and ghee, spices, &c.,
in proportion before the tomb. Hardly is there
time to bake the resulting cakes ere the sky becomes overcast and the worshippers are drenched
to the skin. The Maulana's grandson, Shah Safi,
is the eponymous hero of Sufipur. Many legends
survive to attest his miraculous power. On one
occasion a poor widow, who had lost her all
through the tyranny of the Faujdar of Khairabad,
entreated him to revenge her wrongs. He took
from his mouth the lump of pán which he was
chewing and told her to fix it to an arrow and
shoot it at the house of his oppressor. The

Faujdar, hearing of the advice, ran in great alarm,
prostrated himself at the holy man's feet and
craved and obtained pardon.   Then, from sheer
feminine curiosity the widow shot the *pán* from
a bow at a mound which stood near Khairabad.
The mound at once disappeared and in its place
there opened a yauning gulf which is called to this
day *Safi Sagar*.

The next wave of Mahommedan conquest was
impelled by Sayyid Baharuddin, son of the general who was killed at the battle which led up to the
foundation of Bangarmau.   The Bisseins of Unao
itself fell victims to a notable stratagem planned by
him, full details of which will be found in Sir
William Hunter's monumental *Gazetteer of India,*
in the shape of a quotation from Sir Charles
Elliott's history.   (Vol. xiii p. 428.)   But the
Mahommedan colonies in Unao were not all the
outcome of " blood and iron."   A peaceful invasion of the district resulted from the Moghul
policy of rewarding military service by grants
of land.   These jaghirdars have planted Shaikh
or Sayyid families in nearly every town of any
size: but the only house of any importance—
that of the Rasulabad Sayyids—received its death-
blow during the Mutiny.   The chief then threw
in his lot with the national side, and paid the
penalty of his blunder in the confiscation of his
estates.

Sir Charles's sketch of Unao under Moghul rule is instructive, as proving that the English administration owes but little to the effete organization which it superseded. Under Akbar, when the Government was as strong and highly centralized as imperfect communications admitted, Unao formed a portion of the Lucknow *Sarkar*, the largest of five divisions into which the province of Oudh was split. It contained 14 parganas with a revenue of Rs. 4,52,242, as compared with Rs. 9,63,930 just before the annexation, Rs. 10,33,640 as settled after that event, and Rs. 14,22,720 in 1883-84. Each pargana was administered-by two distinct classes of officials. In the one category came the Qazi, Mufti, Qanungo and Chaudhuri,—generally natives of the pargana and paid by grants of land or fees, and holding their posts for life. The functions of the two first named were judicial. The Qazi was Civil Judge, Registrar, and Priest, with a supervision over the morals and ceremonies of his jurisdiction. The Mufti was a miniature Legal Remembrancer, whose opinion or *futwa* was a necessary basis for the decisions of the Criminal Courts. The duties of the Qanungo and Chaudhuri were connected with the revenue, and they were settlement officers of the pargana. There was no substantial difference between them : but the former appointment was always conferred on the chief zemindar of the pargana ; while the latter fell to a writer of the Kaiesth caste. The second class of officials included the Amil, Krori and Tehsildar. They were seldom residents of the pargana, were often transferred, and were paid either by salary or a percentage on the collections. The Amil was magistrate-collector—the district chief in both revenue and judicial affairs. The Krori and Chaudhuri were subordinate revenue officers; the first taking his name from an obsolete division of the empire into tracts, each paying a crore of *dams*, *i.e.*, two-and-a-half lakhs of rupees. Their duties were identical, and in process of time both merged in the Tehsildar. Above the local officials came the Faujdar, who was military commandant and responsible for the preservation of peace; and the Dewan, whose work was that of general supervision in revenue matters. Higher still there were the officers of the Suba, or province—the Nazim or Governor, the Dewan, or chief Minister, and the Amin, who was responsible for the land settlements. This duality was intended to provide a system of checks and counter-checks, and it survives to this day in many zemindari offices. In practice it worked but indifferently. The history of Unao during the period when the arm of the Emperor of Delhi was longest is a record of rebellion, robbery, murder, and illegal exactions. When the sceptre of Aurungzib fell into impotent hands, the anarchy became intoler-

C

able : and no semblance of order was effected till
Sa'adat Khan, the Nazim of Oudh, threw off his
allegiance and founded the royal house whose last
crowned representative must be fresh in the
memory of Calcutta residents. Sa'adat Khan
was a lineal descendant of Imam Muza Kassim,
of the best blood of Persia. During a civil war
which desolated his native province, Khorassan,
he migrated to Lahore and exchanged his name,
Mir Muhammud Amin, for that which he was
destined to render famous. In 1723 the Emperor
Mahammad Shah created him Subadar of Oudh
with the titles Pillar of the Empire, Confident
Support of the State, Glory of War. Sa'adat
Khan's administration was characterised by a
minute care for his subjects' welfare, which is still
remembered with gratitude. On his death in
1756 he was succeeded by a nephew, Sujaud-
daula, who dropped the title of Subadar and
assumed the loftier one of Nawab Vizier of
Oudh. His grandson, Ghaziuddin Haidar, took
a still bolder flight ; and with the purchased con-
sent of the East India Company became King
of Oudh. During the greater portion of the
Nawabi era, Unao was subject to Faujdars whose
government included the southern portion of
Oudh and the lower Doab. The best of these
functionaries was Ilmas Ali, who flourished at the
end of the last century. He built for himself a town

called Miyanganj, which Sir Charles Elliott styles
one of the few places in Unao worth visiting. It
is a square, with four wide streets meeting in a
central point, surrounded by lofty crenelated
walls, crowned by forty-four towers. Colonel
Sleeman, of Thuggi fame, pays a well-deserved
tribute of admiration to Ilmas Ali, whom he regards as "one of the best and greatest men of
any note that Oudh had produced." "During all
this time," he writes, "Miyan Almas kept the
people secure in life and property, and as happy
as people in such a state of society can be; and
the whole country under his charge was during
his lifetime a garden." What modern Indian
ruler could desire a nobler encomium? The
standard of prosperity was equally high under
King Sa'adat Ali. This vigorous ruler had difficulties in his path which would have taxed the
utmost resources of a Frederic the Great. His
mighty neighbour, the honourable Company, was
in sore straits for money to carry on a series of
wars, great and little; and its demands on the
Garden of India were insatiable. The annual
subsidy exacted rose from £500,000 in 1787 to
£760,000 six years later. In 1801 another turn of
the screw brought up the total to £1,350,000,
and the distracted Sa'adat Ali was fain to purchase immunity from further demands by ceding
half his dominions. He then set himself to the

task of reorganising the administration of the remainder. It was divided into chacklas, of which modern Unao included three entire ones and portion of two more. In every chackla he stationed a strong force of regulars and police to preserve tranquillity and lend the strong arm to the Collectors of revenue at need. The regular troops were paid at the rate of Rs. 4 per mensem, not much more than half the guerdon demanded by the Company's sepoys; and the pay of the police was a rupee less. Thus were life and property in Unao rendered as secure as in the best governed British districts—securer far than in contemporary Bengal. The golden age of the little district was the years between 1740 and 1814, when master-minds such as Ilmas's and Sa'adat Ali's made themselves felt in every branch of the administration. But the native revenue system had inherent defects which brought about its downfall. Sa'adat Ali was a splendid man of business; but he was hard and remarkably close-fisted. Under the Mogul government, and to a less extent that of his immediate predecessors, supervision was lax and local officials made the collection of revenue an excuse for plunder. Sa'adat Ali sought a remedy for this evil in the introduction of the contract system, under which the collections were farmed out yearly to the highest bidders. While he remained

at the helm of affairs, abuses were sternly check-
ed and the mechanism worked smoothly. But he
left behind him no successor capable of compre-
hending his policy in its higher aims, or trained to
seek its continuity. His reforms fell into abey-
ance, and the tide of disorder and oppression rose
higher than ever. The farmers, who were generally mere speculators, were bound to render the
uttermost fraction secured by their bond, and
they could not, and they would not, show mercy to
defaulting proprietors. One class, and one alone,
battened on the general misery. This was the
taluqdars. They were fostered by the revenue
authorities; for the fewer and larger the estates, the
easier it was to realize government dues. Hence
the speedy elevation of the taluqdars on the ruins
of countless smaller proprietors. The cry of the
people rose to heaven ; and if it did not render
annexation inevitable, it at least afforded a reasonable excuse for the active interference of the
British Government. On that much-vexed question our chronicle is judiciously reticent. The
event was too recent when he wrote to be viewed
with the dispassionate judgment which history
demands ; and as an official of the new province,
he probably felt that it would be indecorous to
discuss the question. We of the present day are
on a different stand-point : and this chapter may
fairly conclude with a few words on the annexa-

tion.   In weighing the pros and cons we find it
clear too that neither the British nor the national
party were wholly right or altogether wrong.   The
Nawabi rule was by no means so unspeakably bad
as writers in the interest of the East India Company alleged.   The balance of power between
parties was, in fact, nicely adjusted.   Revenue
must be punctually forthcoming at Lucknow to
gratify the taste for extravagance or miserly hoard-
ing, in which the kings of Oudh indulged.   Hence
the local representatives of Government were
bound, at all hazards, to prevent combination on
the part of taluqdars, and to maintain a conciliatory attitude towards them.   Nor could the latter
afford to quarrel with subordinate holders, for
there were no courts to administer a rigid system
of law without regard for persons.   Hence differ-
ences were generally adjusted by mutual accommodation.   The Nawabi principle, writes Sir
Charles Elliott, was to drive no one to despera-
tion : the English to mete out to every one the
same inexorable justice.   No one who knows India
can doubt which would be most popular in the
country.   The same principle underlay the collection of revenue.   The Government's, and therefore
the zemindars' demands were adjusted to the
produce of the harvests.   The accession of the
English was the signal for a screwing up of revenue to the highest amount ever obtained in

Nawabi times, while payment was rigorously
insisted on whatever were the fluctuations of
agricultural prosperity. It is hardly necessary to
ask which method is best adapted to the easy-
going oriental character. The one feature of the
modern administration which the most inveterate
encomiast of ancient times admits it to excel is
the degree of security afforded to person and
property. But candid native opinion would prefer
that exaction and robbery should be rife, rather
than an unbending law should forbid the indulgence in sacred blood-feuds, and should reduce
great families to ruin in order that money-lenders
might flourish. In the essentials of life and colouring Oudh has undoubtedly lost by the annexation.
Lucknow, while the seat of a Royal court, retained no small share of the glories associated with
oriental rule. Modern India still reeks of the
counting-house, and the sternly-utilitarian spirit
in which government is administered is in itself
enough to account for our failure to win the
people's hearts. Of the political relations between
the Company and the Court of Oudh which led up
to the annexation the less said the better. All
honest Englishmen must look back with humilia-
tion and abhorrence at the duplicity and greed
which marked the intercourse between the Supreme
Government and its old allies, the Subadars of the
Deccan, Bengal, and Oudh. But better times

have dawned. The conscience of England is more acute than it was so lately as 23 years back, when India was saddled with the cost of an official ball given in London to the Sultan of Turkey. Who can doubt that if the Marquis of Lansdowne had been confronted with a situation in Oudh such as that which vexed Lord Dalhousie's soul,* the cradle of Indian Monarchy would have been suffered to remain beneath the sway of a native race?

---

* In a letter to his father written during the throes of the mutiny, Mr. Elliott gave good reason for his belief that the annexation was not distasteful to one class at least whose interests have till lately been deemed beneath the attention of Indian rulers. "Clark and I have ridden out this morning some six miles towards the rebels with a small body of cavalry. As we returned home we crossed a small river, and came over the high ground of its bank. The instant we were seen from the first village, coming from the direction of the rebels, we heard shrieks and cries; every one put his plough to his shoulder and drove his oxen before him—women rushed off into the nearest wood, the whole village was deserted. As we got closer to it, we saw a man lurking about and called to him. He uttered a shout, rushed inside and brought out the zemindar, who came running towards us half laughing. "Oh Saheb!" said he, "We thought you were the rebels!" "What!" I said, laughing, "do I look like a badmash?" "No, saheb," was the reply, "but we could not distinguish, and we took you for Bisram Singh." "The moment they found out we were English the whole village returned at once; and in half an hour twenty ploughs were going merrily again. The same happened with the next village; and returning home we overtook its two zemindars who were on their way to our camp at Burree to tell us that Bisram Singh (a rebel leader of note) had come. I do not hesitate to say the popular feeling is intense desire for our rule among the ryots." (Letter from Mr. C. A. Elliott to the Rev. H. V. Elliott quoted, at pp. 80-81 Gubbins's *Mutinies in Oudh*).

CHAPTER II.

HOSHANGABAD SETTLEMENT.

The Settlement Officer is an evolution of
British rule. The Great Mogul had an elaborate
and not inefficient mechanism for gathering in the
tribute from the land which supported the pomp
and majesty of his court, but this useful func-
tionary found no place therein. From times long
antecedent to the Mahommedan conquest the
State had enjoyed an unquestioned right to a share
in the produce of the soil. This was ordinarily
three-fifths : but the zemindar and village officers
claimed their quota. The first was, in later days
at least, something more than a mere tax-collector.
Offices of all kinds have in India a strong tendency to become hereditary, and, as we shall see
presently, the zemindar had by custom, if not of
right, a first option of re-engaging at the periodical settlements. He was allowed to recoup himself for his risk and trouble by retaining one-tenth
of the Government share, or three-fiftieths of the
gross produce. The village organization had not
yet been crushed beneath the heel of ignorance.
The headman, generally styled *mokaddam,* the
watchman, and the *patwari,* or village accountant,

all took a fixed portion of the collections. The
interests of Government were safeguarded, in
theory at least, by the *canungo,* a representative
of the supreme power, who was in charge of a
group of villages, and submitted reports to the
higher revenue authorities as to the extent and
profits of cultivation, derived from inspection of
the patwaris' accounts. The Provincial head of
the Department, styled *Dewan,* used to summon
the zemindars to a great annual assembly, termed
Punya, at the capital, and offer them a settlement
of the land for the year on terms based on the
canungo's reports. In Bengal these gatherings
were held with much pomp and ceremony at a
fine country seat of the Nawabs Nazim called
Motijhil.* A tradition still lingers in Murshidabad
of the glories of Lord Clive's first *Punya* after
the cession by the titular Emperor of Delhi of
control over the provincial resources.

This sketch of the old revenue system renders it clear that the Settlement Officer was but

---

* "Another point of interest at Murshidabad is the still
beautiful Motijhil, whose deep-blue waters once reflected a stately
palace built by Serajuddaula, which, after the rout of Plassey,
became the chosen residence of Lord Clive. The lake of the pearl
has a special interest in the eyes of Englishmen ; for here in 1765
the cession of the financial control of Bengal, Behar, and Orissa
was solemnly ratified. Thus were the sinews of war provided for
the career of conquest on which our ancestors entered : and thus,
like Runnymede, Motijhil is the cradle of a world-shadowing
empire." F. H. S., in *S. E. Journal.*

faintly foreshadowed in his prototype the canungo of the Moghul era. As the roots of British Empire struck more deeply into the soil, the necessity became clear of employing scientific methods in dealing with the complex problems offered by the administration of land revenue. The work of assessment was no longer left in unskilled and venal hands, but entrusted to the fine flower of the civil and military services. The field of selection was necessarily limited. A Settlement Officer must, in fact, be born one; for the most untiring industry will not compensate for the absence of natural gifts. He must have a minute acquaintance with the farmer's lore—the methods of cultivation, qualities of soil, and cost and value of crops. He should be able to unravel the tangled web of tenure and custom. He must be something of a chemist, botanist, and mathematician. He must have a passion for accuracy and detail, an absorbing love of duties which to the uninitiated seem almost repulsive. If, in addition to these qualities, he has a talent for picturesque description, an eye for the beauties of nature and a warm sympathy with the toiling peasant, we have in him a man fit for a more conspicuous, though not a more useful, rôle than that of assessor to land revenue. It was a small feather in Mr. C. Elliott's cap that the Chief Commissioner of the Central Provinces should have

chosen him at the age of 28 as Settlement Officer
of his richest and most important district.

Hoshangabad is a valley 150 miles in length
between the Nerbudda and the Satpura Hills.
Its area is 4,437 square miles, considerably larger
than that of the English counties of Somerset
and Devon combined.   Its vast expanse of rolling
upland is, for the most part, clothed in due season
with golden corn : for Hoshangabad has a deep,
black soil of inexhaustible fertility and has long
enjoyed the title of the garden of India.   If the
land that has no history is blessed, then Hoshangabad is fortunate indeed.   Until the beginning of
the past century, its annals are well-nigh a blank.
It then became a bone of contention between the
reigning family of Bhopal and the Mahrattas,
with the result which war always brings to the
unhappy peasantry.   Their cup of misery filled
to the brim when the leader of one of the contending factions called in the ruthless Pindaris to
his help.   In 1818, when the greater portion of
the district was taken over by the British Government under treaty with the Peshwa at Nag-
pore, Hoshangabad was a howling desert, dotted
with ruined villages and fields fast relapsing to
jungle.   The process of recuperation which settled
government brings with it was retarded by the
incredible fatuity exhibited in the first settlement
of land revenue made in 1824.   Its author, who

held the title of Political Officer, was one of those
sanguine men who believe that peace and security
attract capital and increased population as if by
magic. Under this impression he raised the revenue of Hoshangabad proper by seventy-three per
cent. in the first year, and so *crescendo* till the
demand for the fifth year was fifty per cent. above
that exorbitant total. The case of Seoni, immor-
talized by Mr. Sterndale's facile pen, was even
worse. The demand there was screwed up from
Rs. 60,000 to Rs. 1,39,000 in five years! The
unhappy zemindars were, of course, unable to
satisfy these claims, and the exactions and cruel-
ties which followed must have made the people
look back on the Pindari raids with something like
regret. The history of the next forty years is a
record of the efforts made to repair this gigantic
blunder. Major Ousley, who reigned supreme as
Principal Assistant Agent to the Governor-General
from 1826 to 1839, brought down the revenue
by 25 per cent, and after 38 years of profound
peace it was still 21 per cent. below that which
was exacted in 1825. Major Ousley appears
to have been a remarkable man: albeit cursed
with that passion for meddling which betrays the
administrator of the second order. He was the
finished type of the patriarchal ruler, and his
regime had all the excellencies and a large share
of the defects inseparable from arbitrary govern-

ment. He lived, says Mr. Elliott, among the people, entertained them in large parties, was a guest at their festivals, and shared in some of their ceremonies. Justice was administered in a simple, untechnical manner, and even the Jail prisoners obtained leave of absence for two or three months together; and, being put on their honor, always came back. But the idyll had the seamy side. Major Ousley's constant interference with the course of business in the supposed interest of the ryot destroyed all confidence and drove capital from the district.* His era left behind it a long train of ills which it needed the reign of law to remove. In 1854 Hoshangabad was placed under a Deputy Commissioner and the North-Western revenue system was introduced in its integrity. From that epoch dates the growth of prosperity which the district has since maintained. The population which, in Major Ousley's time, was only slightly in excess of 200,000, grew to 450,000 in 1871 and 488,000 ten years later.

* In his eagerness to put down oppression on the part of zemindars and money-lenders he forgot the illustrious Turgot's maxim, which should be written in letters of gold in every court-house of the land. " We are sure to go wrong," he used to say, when pressed to confer some benefit on the poor at the expense of the rich, " the moment we forget that justice alone can keep the balance true between all rights and all interests. The key-note to my policy is not pity or benevolence, but justice."

Mr. Elliott's settlement operations commenced in 1863, and his report, a volume of 288 pages with elaborate maps and figured statements, was submitted in 1865 to the Provincial Settlement Commissioner.   It richly merits the encomium passed on it by that officer and the Chief Commissioner, and, indeed, stands unrivalled after a quarter of a century of reports and *nukshas*.   In general plan it is not unlike the author's earlier effort, the *History of Unao*.   The physical features of the district are picturesquely described : and then follows a brief historical sketch.   The general condition of the people is surveyed with a minuteness which proves that Mr. Elliott has that fellow-feeling for toiling humanity in the absence of which the ablest administrator will leave no lasting impression behind him.   Finally, the story of the settlement itself is told in three chapters teeming with information as to tenures, occupancy-rights, waste lands, and a thousand other topics. This portion of the work, though extremely valuable as a record of district administration and a model for future Settlement Officers, is too technical for the great bulk of my readers.   The chapter on the condition of the people is, however, of general interest, and might furnish out not one but half a dozen chapters.   Mr. Elliott's information as to castes is of special value at a time when the bonds of that system are tightening

in the Hindu community.   Ninety-five per cent
of the population of Hoshangabad are, it appears,
Hindu emigrants from Bandelkhand, Marwar, and
Khandesh.   The Gujars are one of the largest
agricultural castes.   Prosperity has altered their
nature, and the thieving, lawless scum of Upper
India has settled down into a community of peaceful farmers, shrewd, vigorous and comparatively
enlightened.   Still more remarkable is the change
which plenty has wrought in the aboriginal Gonds.
According to a contemporary chronicle, they were
sixty years ago "savage and intractable," but
now they are the mildest and most timid of
mortals.   One section into which they are divided,
the Raj-Gonds, have become completely Hindu-
ised.   It is with the Central Provinces as with our
North-Eastern frontier.   The Hindu religion exer-
cises a wonderful fascination for aboriginal tribes.
The glittering bait of caste-recognition induces
the Raj-Gond who has waxed wealthy to don
the *jane* and boast of his Rajput ancestors.
The case of the Rajbanshis is very similar.
They are the most numerous agricultural caste of
Hoshangabad, and also claim a Rajput origin.
But on cross-examination they are fain to admit
that they tarried long on the way.   Strange
to say the Rajbanshis of Northern Bengal are
at this moment agitating for recognition as
Khetris, *i.e.*, Rajputs.   Like their far-away cousins

they are strongly suspected of an aboriginal taint.

The land-owning classes are mostly descendants of officers in the employ of the old lords of the country—the Mussalmans of Bhopal and the Mahrattas of Nagpur. The history of their connection with the soil throws some light on the genesis of zemindars throughout India. If, as was often the case, a cultivating clan is unable to maintain itself till the crops ripened it, or the weaker members at least, must have recourse to some capitalist for a loan. The lender, for his own security, interposes between his debtors and the Government, becomes responsible for the revenue and, armed with the forces of the law, recoups himself by levying rent. Whoever, writes Mr. Elliott, having money by him, came forward at the right time when cultivators were ready to break up the jungle if fed or clothed, that man became the *Malguzar*. The Mahrattas muster strong in this class : and at the time of our report, they owned 29 per cent. of the Hoshangabad villages. They are observant of ritual and but slightly infected with the Marwari shylockism which impairs the dignity of Brahmin immigrants from Hindustan, Rajputana and Bundelkhand. The Mahratta Brahmins differ from their compeers of other provinces in that they marry into any *gotra* but their own : and are sub-divided, not into *kuls*

D

but tribes. The Peshwas belonged to one, and not the highest of their tribes, the Chithans, so called because Parasuram employed their ancestor to perform his father's *Sraddh* which carried with it *Chit*—defilement. A certain proportion of the land, especially in the Seoni pargana, is in the hands of Bunnias; and it is pleasant to find Mr. Elliott saying a good word for a class which is generally held up to execration as blood-suckers. He had not been able to see, he writes, that they were in any respect worse landlords than the rest of the world, less popular or more given to rack-renting.

Our author turns from ethnology to agriculture and adds more to our knowledge of the art as practised in India than all the Agricultural Departments combined have done. The rich black soil will only yield its treasures to assiduous tilling. In May, before the rains set in, it is turned over by a hoe-plough peculiar to these parts, called the *bukhar*, whose iron share weighs three or four seers (7lbs), is 18" to 21" by 4", fixed to a heavy horizontal beam not in line with the furrow, as in the case of the common plough, but at right angles to it. By setting it at a more or less obtuse angle it can be made to pare the weeds at the surface or penetrate the soil to its full depth. This process is repeated at frequent intervals during the rainy months; to *bukhar* in Sraban

(July—August) being imperative. As ·the soil softens under the annual deluge, the *bukhar* penetrates more and more deeply, till the field is purged of weeds, and brought into a condition which would gladden a Midlothian farmer's heart. Its aspect is, however, changed by the invasion of the drill-plough, *nari,* which gets a couple of inches lower down than the *bukhar* and covers the surface of the field with great clods, turned up from a nether stratum. Hence the results obtained in these heavy soils without irrigation. The seed falls into a moist medium and the young shoots spring up through a soft, loosened crest while their roots strike into a sub-soil which has not been caked by exposure to the sun's fierce rays. The system thus described would probably give excellent results in the rich loams so common in Eastern Bengal.

The time of sowing corn depends on the temperature ; for the tender plants would perish if exposed to too great a degree of heat. The ryot has a home-made thermometer, in the shape of a wisp of cotton soaked in *ghee*. This is placed out of doors overnight ; and if the cold has been sufficient to solidify the *ghee,* sowings may be attempted. But astrology and magic are made handmaids to rule of thumb. A lucky day must be fixed upon by the aid of the village priest. In his valuable glossary attached to the report, Mr.

Elliott gives a proverb embodying the folk-lore on the great sowing question,—

" Who ploughs on Sunday shall be rich,
Who ploughs on Monday shall get the fruit of his labour,
Wednesday and Thursday are both good. Friday fills the granary.
Who sows on Saturday or Tuesday no seed shall come to his door."

The end of October and beginning of November are considered *the* season of sowing : and the longer it is deferred the drier and less productive the land. The Hoshangabad farmer is seen at his best at sowing time. He then works for ten or twelve days almost without intermission, and day or night if the moon serves. He never returns home or sleeps more than two or three hours at a stretch. His meals are brought to him in the field by his wife,—wheat chupattis and porridge in abundance. Thus toiling he can plough and sow four-fifths of an acre during day-light and two-fifths on moon-lit nights. More can be accomplished if four or five ploughs work together. Bullocks, like men, are sociable, and it has been remarked that those in the rear of the first pair hardly feel the labour. Would that the wretched, slovenly, dawdling North-Bengal peasant could see his distant brothers at work, for his latent sense of shame might stir him to emulation ! Seed is used in the proportion of a maund of 80 ℔s to the acre. When it is down, the field must be fenced, especially if jungle or high roads be near. The fences are always temporary, mere dry branches of some thorny tree stuck in the ground in line. To make assurance doubly sure, a watchman is engaged by four or five cultivators who club together to pay him 4 maunds of wheat, 320 lbs, per ten acres. He builds a little hut and keeps a bright fire burning. At night he is supposed to walk four times round the field with a blazing branch to scare wild beasts. For royal game he has what is called the "tiger's terror," a drum consisting of an earthen pot covered with a goat's skin well stretched. A peacock's feather is inserted through a hole in the skin and secured with a knot. The watchman holds the pot between his feet and draws his fingers along the feather, eliciting thereby, as Mr. Elliott says, a most unearthly and diabolical sound, which ought to be enough to keep any intelligent beast away.

Wheat ripens towards the end of February, and is cut by Gond and Kurkee immigrants from the hill-country, just as the hay crops of old England were got in twenty years ago by hordes of wild Irishmen from Tipperary and Galway. They usually receive one sheaf in twenty, or if they work in gangs by contract, three maunds (240 lbs.) of wheat per ten acres reaped. The produce averages sixfold,—six maunds, or eight and a half bushels per acre. Threshing and reaping proceed together. The Hoshangabad threshing-floor is not the mere plot cleared of

grass which we see in Lower Bengal. It is well
fenced and provided with a shed for housing
cattle. A short stake is fixed in the centre with
an accompaniment of religious rites, and the wheat
to be threshed is spread round it to a radius equivalent to the length of the line of ten or twelve
bullocks abreast employed to thresh it out. They
are tied to the stake and driven round and round
belly-deep in the golden litter. They are muzzled
at first : but not when the grain has separated and
sunk to the bottom of the pile. Winnowing is
the next operation, and it is hedged about with
ceremonies. An auspicious day for beginning
must be named by the village priest, who is
restricted in his choice by a variety of rules. The
farmer and his labourers will then proceed to the
threshing-floor with the paraphernalia of sacri-
fice,—milk, clarified butter, turmeric and boiled
wheat. These are solemnly offered to the stake,
probably as a survival of Phallic-worship, and to
the heap of threshed grain. The boiled wheat,
etc., are scattered round, to tempt the thieving
bhoots (spirits) away from the former. Then the
master winnows five baskets-full, and the chaff
and grain are collected and measured. If they
fill the baskets, the omen is a good one ; otherwise the spot for winnowing is shifted. These
first-fruits are not added to the heap but are the
perquisite of Brahmins. Winnowing goes on

merrily while a wind is blowing, and employs three
men, one of whom fills the basket, a second
empties it, standing on a stool, while the third
sweeps the grain and chaff into separate heaps.
The day's work is always scrupulously measured
in order to cheat the *bhoots*, who dare not pilfer
when the tale of the wheat is known. Such are
the simple processes by which is produced the
Indian wheat so dreaded by English farmers
and so familiar to frequenters of Mark Lane.
Mr. Elliott considered them fairly well adapted to the conditions prevailing in Hoshangabad. He was at one time an ardent advocate for
the North-Western system of high farming with
irrigation, and inclined to undervalue the primitive
methods which content the peasantry of Hoshangabad. An experiment made by him in 1864 confirm-
ed this view; for he raised a crop of wheat such
as had never been seen in the district from a plot
manured and irrigated *secundum artem*. But
riper knowledge led to a recantation. With an
almost limitless extent of virgin soil awaiting re-
clamation, an area under tillage of three quarters
of a million acres to a population under 450,000,
Hoshangabad had as yet no need to adopt the
scientific methods which are forced on cultivators
elsewhere by the increasing difficulty of gaining
a subsistence. Space fails me to describe the
elaborate experiments undertaken by Mr. Elliott

in view of ascertaining the actual productiveness of the land, the analyses of soils made under his instructions, the minute enquiries into profits and cost of cultivation detailed in this unique volume. One lays it down, with a sigh that there should be so complete a divorce between the Bengal official and the land that supports him. No Settlement Officer in these Provinces could hope for Mr. Elliott's opportunities of penetrating the veil that conceals the peasant's life. They must be content to wear the best years of their life away in a dull and ever-increasing drudgery of routine reports, bundles and figured-statements; and, the great book of nature, the short and simple annals of the poor, are alike shrouded from their view.

CHAPTER III.

THE FAMINE COMMISSION.

Mr. Elliott's splendid work for Hoshangabad was rewarded by Sir William Muir by an appointment as Secretary to the Government of the North-Western Provinces. One of the most serious obstacles to the perfect success of our regime is the fact that the Secretariats, which are the mainsprings of the administration, have been so largely composed of men devoid of experience in the great world's ways and the microcosm afforded by the district. Mankind is not governed by bundles. On the other hand, it is difficult to overrate the advantage, both to the individual and the community, of Secretariat experience gained when the judgment is ripe and some insight has been attained into the motives of human action and the mechanism of society. Mr. Elliott's intimate knowledge of Indian character and customs stood him in good stead in this new post, carrying him far above the soul-depressing files and dockets in which so many Secretaries are content to wallow. His broad sympathies with fellow-creatures led him to enter on a crusade against the hideous practice of infanticide among Rajput clans. In official routine he inaugurated

some useful reforms. He it was who set the
principle of testing Police work by the percentage
borne by convictions to cases reported, and established a wholesome rivalry amongst District staffs
by arranging them in a varying order of merit. On
him devolved the superintendence of the Census
of 1871-2 in the North-West, a task the difficulty of which his colleagues who have passed
through the ordeal of 1891 may be able to appreciate.

After a brief period spent in 1877 in the
" general line " as Commissioner of the Mirat
Division, Mr. Elliott had the opportunity for which
so many able men sigh and sigh in vain, of proving his mettle by a crucial test. A terrible famine
broke out in Southern India ; and officers gifted
with organizing power and exhaustless energy
were needed to direct the operations for relief.
Mr. Elliott was named, jointly with Sir C. Mon-
crieff, to serve as Famine Commissioner in Mysore.
In the following year the scope of his labours was
enlarged by the formation of a Famine Commission for the purpose of investigating the causes of
these terrible visitations and prescribing reme-
dial action. He became Secretary to that body ;
and it is no disparagement to his associates to
affirm that his hand is evident in nearly every
page of the four large blue-books in which their
report was laid before the British Parliament. His

work in this sphere has had more far-reaching
consequences than any performed during a long
and busy career : and we must linger awhile in
describing its scope.

The instructions given by the India Office
to the Famine Commission were as vague as most
of the utterances of that official Delphi. They
were, however, amplified by the Government of
India in a minute penned with a statesmanlike
breadth. The Commission were to ascertain how
far local peculiarities of administration, tenure,
soil, water-supply, density of population, and systems of cultivation tend to intensify or mitigate
famine. They were to gauge the comparative
power of the agricultural population in different
Provinces to resist the effects of drought, their
relative wealth, and the relation of their well-being
to the varied forms of land tenure. As regards
the species of relief to be afforded, the battle of
large against small and scattered works was to
be fought to the bitter end. The Commission
were told to point out the limitations to the duty
of Government in the matter of food-supply.
They were to discuss the influence of forests and
irrigation on food. The great question of transit
was to be threshed out : how far road and water
carriage were susceptible of improvement ; how
the blocks on railways resulting from abnormal
pressure on staff and rolling-stock might be mini-

mized. The financial responsibility for famine relief was to be defined. Finally, its whole mechanism in every shape must be scrutinized and, if necessary, remodelled. The programme was one which must have appalled even such a glutton for work as the future Lieutenant-Governor of Bengal : but he set about the task of perform-ance with characteristic ardour. A series of in-terrogatories was framed and circulated to officials with special experience and others whose position had brought them in close contact with the Indian people. The replies elicited fill nearly a thousand closely-printed pages of foolscap size. This•mass of information was supplemented by personal experience gained in visits paid to nearly every Province. The question of irrigation as a pro-phyllactic was so large as to necessitate the appointment of a special committee who travers-ed the regions watered by canals and considered on the spot the various problems they offer. The report is in two parts, with as many bulky volumes of evidence. The first part deals with relief : the second with measures of protection and preser-vation. The curtain rises with a geographical sketch of the peninsula which brings into clear relief the conditions tending to produce famine. Its primary cause is drought,—an abnormal cessa-tion of the rains at the period when the great winter rice crops is approaching maturity. The tracts most liable to famine are those with an annual rainfall ranging between 30 and 35 inches. Famines have occurred at varying intervals since the dawn of civilization : but the earliest of which we have any detailed record devastated Bengal in 1770-1. There is too much reason to believe that this famine was intensified by the callous greed of certain high officials and their understrappers who formed a "ring," as we should call it now-a-days, for the purpose of raising the price of grain. A third of the population of the Lower Provinces, then estimated to contain thirty million souls, is believed to have perished. In 1784 scarcity ravaged Upper India, which, if less destructive to life, was far more widely felt. In 1807 Madras was a sufferer, and then for the first time we see some recognition of the principle that the adoption of relief measures is incumbent on Government. Large remissions of land revenue were granted and loans were made to landed proprietors. It was sought to stimulate private trade by bounties on grain imported and guaranteeing a minimum price to importers. A further step in advance was made in 1837-8, when the Upper Provinces and the adjoining Native States suffered grievously from a failure of their crops. The principle was then laid down that employment must be provided for able-bodied sufferers by Government ; while the maintenance of the helpless was primarily a charge on private charity. Public works which cost twenty lakhs of rupees were set on foot, and relief committees were organized in each district to administer funds derived from public subscriptions, supplemented by State grants. Thirty years passed by without a serious failure of the crops ; and our rulers had begun to flatter themselves that the spectre of famine had been laid. Their optimism received a rude shock in May 1866 when the discovery was suddenly made that the markets throughout Orissa were depleted. Ere supplies could be furnished the monsoon set in, cutting off access by sea ; while the only land communication available was an unmetalled road which each rainy season made a quagmire. The peasantry died off by hundreds of thousands, and the mortality was only stayed in November when the Bengal Government, rushing from the extreme of apathy to that of unreasoning panic, poured forty thousand tons of rice into the country, much of which was sold for a mere song.

This prodigality was repeated on a vaster scale in Behar, where acute distress followed the failure of the autumn rain in 1873. Sir Richard Temple, who then occupied the Belvedere *gadi*, saw in this calamity an outlet for his almost superhuman activity. He laid it down as an axiom that in times of famine private trade was but a broken reed to lean on ; and that it was

incumbent on Government to prevent mortality
and distress at all costs. With this end in view
nearly half a million tons of grain were imported,
mostly from Burma, and distributed by way of
loans to agriculturists from depôts scattered over
Behar. The landless class were enabled to earn a
liberal grain wage on what were euphemistically
termed relief works; but the tests exacted were
little more than nominal, and, in point of fact, the
staff of life was distributed freely to all comers.
In fine, a quarter of the population of Behar was
supported for several months at a cost to the State
of six and a half millions sterling, much of which
went to swell the gains of middlemen. But for
the self-reliance and self-respect inherent in the
Indian character the entire fabric of society would
have received a fatal shock. Far different was
the fate of sufferers in the Madras Presidency
during the famine which followed a drought in
1876 and an irregular monsoon in the following
year. At the very outset much precious time
was wasted owing to a difference of opinion between the Supreme and the Local Government as
to the character of the relief works which should
be set on foot. The first preferred small and
scattered ones, bringing relief home to every
man's door: the second strenuously advocated
large and highly centralized operations. Taught
by the bitter experience gained in Behar the

Government of India impressed on its subordinates that while no pains were to be spared to save life, it was futile to aim at the prevention of all suffering. Everyone is agreed on the folly and worse of indiscriminate private charity; but the fact often escapes recognition that the evil is multiplied a thousandfold when Government is the offender. The maxim is unimpeachable; but it must have been due to a sense of humour unsuspected in so august a body that led Lord Lytton's Council to despatch Sir Richard Temple to preach the new Gospel in the benighted South. The Madras famine, however, set economy at defiance and cost the State eight and a half million sterling.

The inferences to be drawn from past history are set forth with great precision in Mr. Elliott's report. We must be prepared, it seems, to face a scarcity with partial distress in some portion of the Empire in two years out of nine, and a famine once in twelve years. Every province may expect drought with its inevitable result once in eleven or twelve years; and a great famine twice in a century. The greatest number ever likely to be simultaneously afflicted is thirty millions. As distress or plenty varies directly with the harvests, it is well to know that a peasant who gathers in half an average crop can 'scrape along' till the earth shall again yield her increase :

but famine becomes a certainty when the produce falls below a quarter of that of an ordinary year. Taking price as a criterion we find that when rice sells at eight to ten seers per rupee, the danger signal must be considered as hoisted; but material conditions vary so enormously that the price-test is not of universal application.   The direct mortality from famine is by no means so great as is commonly supposed—far less, in fact, than that resulting from epidemics which often occur in times of plenty; but distress undoubtedly impairs fecundity and causes a drop in the birth-rate.   It is, cheering to learn that India has a marvellous recuperative power; and that famines show a tendency to become less acute in modern times.

Turning from cause to effect, Mr. Elliott's Commission laid it down as a fundamental dogma that the battle with famine lies within the scope of the duties of an Indian Government; first, because such calamities transcend all private effort, and secondly because the State is here the landlord.   But the interference of Government must be beneficial, and not such as to check the operations of thrift and self-reliance.   Indian Society rests on the ties of family and village; and these primitive organizations, combined with the national frugality and foresight, enable it to resist a strain which would ruin communities more highly developed.   The first symptoms of famine are never

E

shown by the enormous class which tills its own land ; for it has resources in the shape of stocks or credit which enable it to hold out for several months, perhaps, even to tide over the crop-failure. It is the landless labourer, the artizan and small trader, the beggar, the cripple and the leper, the dependent on a family well-to-do in ordinary times, who feel the first pangs of want. Candidates for relief are ranged in two classes—those who are incapable of work and those from whom some form of labour may be exacted. In the case of the first it is of great importance that the inception of relief works should not be too long delayed for then the constitutions of the distressed may be fatally enfeebled. It is, therefore, essential that a list of public works to be undertaken in the event of famine should be prepared in each district in advance. These might be connected with roads, drainage or water supply and should be placed in as close proximity as possible to the habitations of the distressed. The " distance test " as it is called, *i.e.* insistence on candidates for employment traversing a certain distance in search of work, is condemned, and very rightly so, by the Commission. They object, too, to the intervention of the contractor, while admitting that a gang or two of the more able-bodied might be employed on piece work. Organization and control should rest primarily on trained Engineers under the general supervision of the District Collector. The task exacted should be seventy-five per cent. of that rendered by a labourer in ordinary times; the dole, whether in grain or money, should be such as to furnish subsistence to the labourer and his helpless dependents. The case of those unable to work is to be met by alms, distributed, as far as possible, in village centres through the duly-controlled agency of village officers. The camp and poor-house-organizations with which it was sought to stem the tide of famine in Madras are open to grave and radical objections. It is our primary duty to preserve the mechanism of village and family intact. The principle in dealing with the great question of food supply is non-interference with private trade, save in such exceptional cases as a combination among dealers to raise prices, or communications so defective as to deter enterprize. Then and then only should the State intervene and import grain into famine-stricken tracts. That old-fashioned nostrum for famine, the storing of grain in times of plenty, is utterly futile in dealing with the vast population of Upper India. In this respect the duty of Government is to watch over the course of trade, and facilitate it by providing communications and canals. Minor, but still important, measures of relief are the grant of remissions of revenue and loans to the landed classes. The first should be made conditional on similar concessions being made to the peasantry. In regard to the second, the Behar Famine of 1874 elicited the fact that advances by Government are faithfully repaid, and involve small risk of financial loss. They should be devoted primarily to the purchase of bullocks and seed grain. Lastly, the responsibilities of local bodies—Municipalities and District Boards—as to co-operation in Famine prevention and relief must be declared and defined with strictness. The chain of official subordination in relief measures, should range from the Head of the Administration through a new Department to be termed that of the Director of Agriculture and Famine relief, Commissioners of Divisions, District officers, those in charge of Circles or groups of villages, down to the village headmen. In order to secure uniformity of procedure, a draft Famine Code was submitted by the Commission. It needs but a superficial acquaintance with the public measures of the decade which has followed this epoch-making report to recognize the fact that nearly every recommendation it contained has been adopted by the Indian Government. Would that the work of the Commissions which succeed each other as winter does the scorching heats were as pregnant of great and lasting results !

CHAPTER IV

THE ADMINISTRATION OF ASSAM.

Mr. Elliott's labours on the Famine Commission had scarcely terminated ere he was called to functions equally onerous in connection with the Indian Census of 1881. As Commissioner he organized the victory won by less conspicuous agents over the blind forces of ignorance and prejudice. In this capacity he visited every province with the exception of Assam during the cold weather of 1880-81, leaving the task of tabulation and report to his successor, Sir W. Plowden. He became Chief Commissioner of Assam in March 1881 in the room of Sir Steuart Bayley, translated to the Residency of Hyderabad. Some of our so-called non-regulation provinces seem to exist mainly to serve as stepping-stones to the Bengal *gaddi*. There the future Lieutenant-Governor may linger awhile and try his prentice hand on material more suited to experiments in the art of governing than our own. Not that Assam is devoid of complex problems. It is cut off from our railway system; inhabited by a sturdy race of European settlers who are proverbially less amenable to discipline than are the children of the soil; and hemmed in on three

sides by vast highlands peopled by tribes ranging
in point of social development between the un-
redeemed savagery of the Lushais and the semi-
civilization of Manipur and Tipperah. In the
year prior to Mr. Elliott's advent to power a high
British officer had been inveigled into a trap by
the Angami Nagas and massacred with the greater
portion of his escort. Nor is the danger to public
peace confined to the belt of frontier tribes. Soon
after Mr. Elliott's arrival a serious rising took
place in the old-settled district of Cachar. A
certain Sumbhudan set up as a god and pretend-
ed to convey a divine afflatus to many deluded
followers. So unbounded became his influence
that none could be found to serve a process on
him. The Deputy Commissioner who endeavoured to bring these fanatics to reason was charged
furiously by them and received a wound which
caused his death. Mr. Elliott's policy towards his
dangerous neighbours during his term of office
in Assam was one of conciliation coupled with
firmness. The practice of wholesale village-
burning which had hitherto served as a punish-
ment for raids was discouraged : but the frequent
incursions of these tribes into British territory,
generally undertaken in order to bring back re-
fugees to allegiance, were sternly repressed. To
the tact and vigilance displayed during his four
years' tenure of office may be ascribed the ab-

sence of serious outrages on our North Eastern frontier.

Turning to internal administration we find that this once backward province owes to Mr. Elliott the large measure of self-government she enjoys. On the basis of Lord Ripon's famous circular of May 1882 he framed a scheme for entrusting the people with the management of their own public affairs. Boards, charged with the supervision of roads and schools, were organized in every district. In Kamrup and Sibsagar, once the seats of government and still possessing a strong leaven of influential families, the Native members of these boards were elected by the whole body of ryots paying revenue to government. In Sylhet, which is virtually part and parcel of Bengal, the Deputy Commissioner nominated an elective body consisting of a local notable residing in each census circle, which, in its turn, selected representatives on the board. Elsewhere the native members were nominees of government; but where the tea-planting interest predominated, as it did in five of the eight plains' districts, half the non-official members were elected by vote from this class. The influence of officialism was restricted by a proviso that its representatives should in no case exceed one third of the total. All means were taken of increasing the Boards' prestige and interesting them in their work. The Executive Engineer had hitherto been independent of the civil officer, and treated as a separate and equal authority. The resulting friction ceased when he was placed under the Deputy Commissioner, and afterwards under the Boards with the title of District Engineer. Some idea of the utility of these new bodies may be gathered from the fact that the expenditure on public works, including two short lines of railway, rose from ten lakhs in 1879-80 to twenty-six during Mr. Elliott's last year of office in Assam : and that Rs. 2,84,000 was devoted to maintaining 1,200 schools during the year first mentioned as compared with Rs. 4,50,000 in keeping up 1,800 schools at the later epoch. The benefits to the planting community from the large outlay on roads and bridges has been incalculable. Nor was this the only advantage desired by it from Mr. Elliott's view of the importance of improving methods of locomotion. Assam had always been terribly handicapped by her antiquated system of river traffic. The journey between Calcutta and Sibsagar was made in large steamers, each towing a pair of cumbrous flats ; and often occupied a longer time than that from England to the Metropolis. Planters were therefore cut off from the cheerful ways of man as effectually as the Britons of old from Roman civilization : and a profound stagnation overspread the province. To Mr.

Elliott it owed the establishment of the fast daily
mail service on its great rivers which has done
more than aught besides to bring Assam within
the pale of progress. But if its principal trade
was hampered by defective communications it was
not less so by well-meaning but mischievous legislation. The labour question is a burning one with
Assam planters. To hold their own against the
fierce competition of China and Ceylon they must
have coolies on reasonable terms: and their
efforts in that direction were thwarted by the
operation of laws and rules which appeared to
have been framed in view of discouraging emigration from less sparsely populated districts. The
Inland Emigration Act of 1882 introduced four
drastic changes in principle. It promoted free
emigration; gave preference to recruitment by
garden agents over recruitment by contractors;
raised the maximum period for which contracts
could be made from three to five years: and
legalized such contracts within the province itself.
Under these fostering influences the production of
tea rose from thirty-one million pounds in 1879-80
to fifty-one million in 1883-4 an increase of 60
per cent. in four years.

The interests of the native population of
Assam were not less considered by Mr. Elliott.
He paid yearly visits to every District and nearly
every Sub-division of his extensive charge, and

ascertained local wants by personal conference with the members of the various boards. District officers were specially enjoined to do likewise. In a resolution which foreshadowed those orders issued in October last which have evoked so much criticism in official circles, he imposed on these subordinates the duty of spending at least four months of each year in the interior of their charges. This prolonged sojourn in tents was, he said, rendered possible by the Assam climate, whose mildness in mid-April is in sharp contrast with the intolerable heat of early summer in other provinces. The revenue-law of Assam had been in state bordering on chaos. Every variety of organization known to India was at work : and the confusion was more confounded by an absence of system in attempts to deal with the numerous difficulties attending on land administration. Mr. Elliott's Code, founded on a draft originally prepared by Mr. W. Ward when Judge and Commissioner, simplified the process immensely. He remodelled the subordinate collecting agency by substituting tehsildars, as seen in the North-Western Provinces, for the *mauzadars*, or revenue contractors who had oppressed the cultivator and intercepted a large share of the revenue. The future of the waste lands, amounting, in the Assam valley alone, to nine million of acres, occupied his close attention. These were not, as he remarked in the Administration Report for 1881-2, overgrown with forests, but good, flat, alluvial soil, covered only with grass and reeds which required nothing but the sickle and the match to turn them into excellent ash manure : while the abundance of bamboo and cane made the building of a comfortable hut the work of a few days. This settler's paradise awaited occupants principally because the absence of any limit to appropriations favoured the growth of a squatter-community similar to that which has so greatly hindered the legitimate expansion of our Australian Colonies. Mr. Elliott took the first step towards the destruction of these monopolies by ordaining that no grant should in future exceed 600 acres : and that the cultivation of a grant should be a condition precedent to any further concessions. In 1883 a survey was commenced of waste lands in the Lakhimpur District, which was carried out by a private firm at the cost of grantees. No fewer than 134,000 acres were thus demarcated in three years. Those who are familiar with Sir C. Elliott's recent utterances will be prepared to learn that he attached great importance to such operations while in Assam. In 1882 he formed a special department, the Directorate of Agriculture, for the purposes of systematic surveys ; and thus anticipated events in Bengal by nearly two years. The first task undertaken by the new

Director was the cadastral survey of 228 square miles in Kamrup at a cost of only 6 as. 9 pie per acre. In 1884-5 a further area of 450 square miles was thus treated. In order to provide the necessary staff for the maintenance of the splendid cadastral maps, seven survey schools were opened which imparted technical instruction to officers employed on this duty and issued certificates of proficiency.

There was, indeed, no branch of the administration from which Mr. Elliott's reforming hand was absent. In the management of the Excise, for instance, it had been the practice to let ,the, exclusive rights of opening shops in a given area for the vend of spirits, *ganja* and opium. This system favoured the growth of middlemen; for the purchasers invariably sublet the shops within their *mahals*, as they were called, and thus intercepted a large proportion of the profits which should have enriched the exchequer. Mr. Elliott directed that all shops should be let directly by government; and partly by this change and partly by judicious enhancement of the selling price of stimulants he raised the excise revenue from eighteen and a half to twenty-two lakhs in three years.

We have seen enough of Mr. Elliott's Administration in Assam to recognize its fundamental maxim. It was justice for the children of the soil; justice for the European settler; justice for the government he served. It was thus with the illustrious Turgot, when governor of a province of old France before the Revolution. The key-note to his policy, writes a biographer, was not pity or benevolence, but justice. "We are sure to go wrong he said," when pressed to confer a benefit on the poor at the expense of the rich, "the moment we forget to hold the balances true amongst all claims and all interests." Such must be the watch-word of our Empire wherever Britain's flag waves on the breeze, if we would .avoid a cataclysm such as wrecked the proudest monarchy of Europe and shook the whole fabric of civilization.

CHAPTER V

THE FINANCE COMMITTEE.

The decentralization of finance was, perhaps, the most beneficent measure of Lord Mayo's brief regime. Up to his time the provincial governments had dipped at their own sweet will into the imperial exchequer; and extravagance with its inevitable results was universal. In 1871 came into force that which is known as the contract system; by which local governments were allotted, certain definite sums to cover the charges of the chief departments under them, and were informed that any excess on the debit side of their ledger must be covered by local taxation. The weak point in this scheme was the inelasticity of the resources placed at the disposal of the provincial authorities. This inconvenience was remedied in 1878 by the assignment to them of the revenue derived from certain branches of the administration such as excise, stamps, law and justice, and the like: the Supreme Government reserving to itself a share only in the future increase of revenue under these heads. This statesmanlike measure infused new life into the dry bones of provincial administration. Satraps had now for the first time a direct interest in economy and the development of their resources. From the epoch of the contract system dates that steady expansion of our revenues which has enabled the exchequer to meet the heavy losses entailed by the depreciated rupee. The term of the contracts between the Imperial and Local Governments is five years ; that entered into in 1882 expiring in 1887. To facilitate the impending reorganization of finances Lord Dufferin, in March 1886, appointed a Committee of experts with power to scrutinize the Expenditure of every department of the Empire and to suggest large economies. Mr. Elliott's vast experience of similar functions pointed him out as the man of all others for the direction of this enquiry. He was, therefore, named Chairman of the Committee. With him were associated Sir Henry Cunningham, Sir W. Hunter, the Hon'ble M. Ranade, Colonel Filgate and Messrs. T. Westland, Bliss and Hardie. The Committee's preliminary labours were facilitated by the appointment of Sub-committees to deal with the various departments. Printed notes were drawn up summarizing the information required and suggestions received, and were circulated among departmental chiefs. On receipt of replies to these, all persons responsible for expenditure were invited to confer with the Committee and clear up points of doubt. Visits were paid by delegates from the Committee to the head quarters of each government : and strenuous efforts were made to digest and systematize the enormous mass of details within the limited period allowed by the Government of India. The task proved impossible of fulfilment : and, in December 1886 the Committee submitted a report which was necessarily incomplete. It is comprised in two folio blue-books of nearly a thousand pages. The first part relates to the forthcoming contracts for 1887, and the second to departmental and miscellaneons expenditure. To follow the Committee through the labyrinth of facts and figures in which their enquiries are recorded would require a volume ; and it is to be feared that my readers would find it as imbued with " disgusting dryness " as Bishop Burnet did the *magnum opus* of Lord Clarendon. That which shines conspicuous throughout is Mr. Elliott's amazing power of manipulating figures and his capacity for entering into details. His conclusions were not accepted without demur from some of his colleagues : Sir H. Cunningham and Mr. Ranade being conspicuous in the extent and number of their protests. A large majority, however, were accepted by the supreme government : and the contracts which are now about to expire were based on the Committee's recommendations. The annual gain to the Indian exchequer by the economies suggested was, in round figures Rx. 1,280,000—nearly a million sterling at the rates of exchange then current. In the course of 1887 the threads laid down by the Committee were taken up by Mr. Elliott in the capacity of Finance Commissioner with the Government of India; and a blue-book of 660 pages compiled by him discusses the subjects untouched by the defunct Committee. The insight which the three volumes afford into the mechanism of administration in British India leads us to question the universal applicability of Count Oxenstiern's views as to the little wisdom shown in the art of government. We are most of us too prone to accept the noiseless working of the state machine as a matter of course; and to ignore the vast amount of skill and labour it involves, while we lay the utmost stress on the failures which must beset the course of every human institution. Mr. Elliott's Committee dragged many anomalies and some abuses to the light of day. It is tolerably certain, however, that no other empire in the world has less to conceal or would have borne so successfully a piercing scrutiny.

Hardly had Mr. Elliott completed this task ere he was called upon by Lord Dufferin to assume the portfolio of Public Works Minister, for such *de facto* is the Member of Council who has this great department in his charge. Every high official who has illustrated this office has had his peculiar hobby. Mr. Elliott's bent lay strongly

F

towards our railway system. There was doubt-less much in its complicated mechanism and the immense variety of economic questions which its working involves that appealed to his severely practical mind and to his instincts as a born administrator. Hardly had he taken his seat in Council than he threw himself with characteristic vigour into the great controversy of private *versus* public enterprize in railways. The question is destined to exert so vast an influence on the his-tory of civilization that a brief retrospect of its phases may not be out of place. England, the mother of railways, was at the time of their birth permeated with the doctrine of *laissez-faire*. Statesmen and economists were for the most part agreed that the function of the state stop-ped at the preservation of order, and that the fullest scope should be given to the impulse they were pleased to term "enlightened self-interest." There was much in our past history which justi-fied this view. Our commerce, and indeed our Empire itself, had been the slow evolution of private enterprize. Hence an inactivity which was the reverse of masterly characterized the attitude of the state towards the wondrous discovery. The right of constructing new lines was allowed to become a bone of contention between rival promoters, whose struggles for vic-tory in the courts and before Parliamentary

Committees increased three-fold the initial cost of our railways and has left England with a system, marred by many serious defects. Our example was followed by the United States, where 160,000 miles of railways are in the hands of 600 private companies. With few exceptions the lines are exploited by unscrupulous wirepullers who pile up vast fortunes at the expense of a long-suffering public. In Italy the Government has endeavoured to keep private enterprize under some control by granting concessions to competing lines throughout the length of the peninsula: but it is understood that most of them have combined against the common enemy—the traveller, the merchant and the producer. The springs of authority are stronger in France ; and the state has reserved to itself the option of purchasing many existing lines, which are at present under private management. French railways are proverbial for combining a maximum of charges with a minimum of speed and accommodation. In northern and central Europe, on the other hand, the state, from motives connected with strategy, has retained a firm grip on the railway network. The result has fully justified this policy. The zone system, by which railways having termini at a common centre are divided into sections over which coaching and goods charges are identical, must revolutionize the working of lines throughout the world. Its success has been demonstrated in Austro-Hungary, and it is only possible where railways are owned by the state. Though much diversity of practice still prevails, public opinion is slowly veering round towards the theory that the enormous powers now necessarily vested in companies can only be successfully wielded by the governing power. The splendid success of our postal and telegraph system has opened men's eyes to the advantage of state control over methods of inland locomotion. We are beginning to doubt the wisdom of the old war-cries. Enlightened self-interest is often synonymous with selfishness; and *laissez-faire* with a criminal abnegation of the first duty of a state—the protection of the weak against knavery and strength. Mr. Elliott, therefore, was in sympathy with modern thought when he pronounced strongly against the surrender of our Empire to the railway promoters. A patient trial had indeed been given to private management and it had been found wanting. All the conditions necessary for economical working were absent. Minute division of responsibility and close supervision are the A.B.C. of railway management. Neither was possible with Boards of Directors sitting 6,000 miles away; always readier to gain the good-will of their subordinates by sanctioning extravagant expenditure, than to seek the best interests of their shareholders.

" Enlightened self-interest " in railway management takes the form of unfair competition, of
such devices as the lowering of junction rates in
order to block rival lines, and of endeavours made
to drive traffic into the longest " lead." The
injustice thus involved cannot be remedied by
state control. An attempt was made in that
direction in 1887, when it was sought to impose
on the principal companies a schedule of uniform
maxima and minima goods' rates. It was frus-
trated by a declaration on the part of the E. I. R.
authorities to the effect that they reserved to
themselves the right of varying the classification
as their interests might demand. Two years
later a fierce contest began between that line
and the new Indian Midland. The Cawnpore
traffic was the aim of each ; and the former
company sought by every means in its power
to force it through the longer ' lead,' *viâ* Jabal-
pur. The Government, after taking the opinion
of eminent counsel, declined to interfere for the
protection of exporters. During the term of office
of Sir Charles Elliott (he had at last obtained
the long deserved distinction of K.C.S.I.) a half-
hearted step in the direction of control was forced on the Indian government by the home authorities. Under instructions from the Secretary of
State an Act (1 of 1890) was passed which provided for the appointment of a commission to

settle disputes between rival companies. It is very doubtful, however, whether this imitation of English practice will be aught but a dead letter in India. The companies here can fall back on their contracts and evade compliance with any decision at which a commission might arrive as regards rates. One is driven to the conclusion that the State can exercise no efficient control over a vast commercial railway in private hands. Companies must be suffered to prey on each other or combine against the public till the evil grows too great for bearing. The question of the construction of railways is intimately connected „with their management. Our policy in this respect was, till Sir Charles Elliott's regime, marked by a singular absence of consistency, and, indeed of common sense. The older lines were built on loans in the English market raised by the glittering bait of a gold guarantee so heavy that shareholders were content to rest on their oars, certain that, whether their lines were well or ill managed, the capital invested would always bring a handsome return. Though this system has been justly exploded the interests of the tax-payer have been, on more than one occasion of late years, sacrificed by the transfer of new lines to private management on most inequitable terms. When the Council were allowed a free hand, as in the case of the purchase of the Oudh and Rahilkhand and the construction of the Amballa-Kalka lines, a far better bargain has been secured. Sir Charles Elliott's attitude as regards construction was logical enough. With the completion of the East Coast and the Assam-Chittagong lines, the trunk system of this Empire will be fairly complete; and branches, or feeders, will alone remain to be embarked on. It is preferable that such works should be undertaken by the government or by public bodies under governmental control on capital borrowed with the Secretary of State's guarantee. But the interest must be payable in silver and the guarantee must not exceed three per cent. If private promoters are willing to accept these terms there is abundant room for them; for government has its hands full, and the new-fledged public bodies have at present neither the means nor the knowledge to fit them for great enterprizes. The function of the constructors must, however, cease with the completion and equipment of the new lines. Experience has shown that trunks can work branches more economically than the latter can work for themselves. Therefore feeders should be leased out to lines with which they are connected at a fixed proportion of their gross earnings. Fifty per cent is a ratio which is fair to all concerned.

The battle of the gauges is a minor phase of the railway controversy. The broad gauge, so called—5′ 6″—is that which finds most favour at home : and it has been adopted on most of our trunk lines. Without pronouncing positively for the metre gauge, or underrating the evils of a break, Sir Charles Elliott, to judge from his public utterances, looks with favour on a system which favours extreme cheapness of construction and protects the permanent way from the wear and tear of heavy engines and high speeds. The question of breaks is another burning one in the railway world. After directing a series of elaborate experiments Sir Charles Elliott has pronounced in favour of the Vacuum break, influenced by its greater simplicity and the power it possesses of bringing a train to a complete stop without the intermittency in working needed in the case of its rival, the Westinghouse. These breaks have, therefore, been fitted to all the N. W. R. trains and to those on the E. B. S. and Oudh and Rohilkhund which carry mails. Here, at least, government management is in advance of that of any private company in India.

But Sir Charles is something more than a mere theorist. Besides formulating a policy to govern the relations of the state with railway enterprize he devoted close personal attention to the development of the net-work of lines. Projects embracing 1064 miles of permanent way, begun before his term of office, were completed during its course. Twelve lines, aggregating 596 miles, were carried through from their inception. Nine, including 1671 miles, were begun but were unfinished when he vacated his seat in Council. Surveys in 18 more projects were ordered; and in 12 of them the plans and specifications were ready at the close of his functions as public works minister.

Though railways were evidently Sir Charles's hobby, the interests of their rivals, the canals were not neglected. Two new systems came under construction. The first is the Peryar Canal in the Madras Presidency; a splendid work from an engineering point of view, but one which is not likely to bring a larger area than at present under cultivation. The second is that known as the Sirsa and Chenab Canal. The Panjab alone of Indian Provinces possesses every factor necessary to the success of artificial waterways. It is a dry and thirsty land, in spite of its historic rivers. Good water runs to waste, while acres untold lie fallow for want of it. The sturdy peasantry have turned their spears to ploughshares, and bring to bear on cultivation the dogged determination with which they once fought for the Khalsa. In Bengal proper, with the sole exception of South Behar, irrigation by means of canals has been a failure. Other provinces are either well provided already or enjoy climatic condition which render canals

G

superfluous. That the grand scheme connected with the Jhelam, which has been surveyed and has received the sanction of the Secretary of State, should still hang fire in the absence of allotted funds is deeply to be regretted in the interests of Upper India.

The personal equation is of the first import-ance to the smooth working of so vast a depart-ment as that of Public Works. When Sir Charles Elliott took his seat in council the civil branch was seething with discontent. Loud complaints were heard on all sides of retarded promotion and undue preference shown to Royal Engineers. The first grievance is a very real one. No attempt had ever been made to ascertain the strength at which the staff of engineers must be maintained, or to adjust recruitments. The wildest guesses at Indian requirements were made: and when Cooper's Hill College was set on foot the annual supply of young Civil Engineers was fixed at fifty. In 1874 no fewer than eighty were launched on an Indian career. Sir Charles Elliott's enquiries as to the real needs of all branches of the P. W. D. resulted in placing it beyond all doubt that the staff, exclusive of the military works branch, should be kept down to 730 officers; 600 of whom should be civil engineers. Actuarial computations proved that twenty-four men were required annual-ly to fill vacancies caused by deaths and retirements among the latter. Half of these will in future be supplied by Cooper's Hill and half by Indian colleges or recruited from deserving subordinates. Under this arrangement the utility of Cooper's Hill appears open to grave doubt. The Indian tax-payer has every right to protest against the maintenance of an expensive establishment at home which turns out a dozen young engineers annually. A vast impetus would be given to technical education in this country were twelve additional appointments in the upper grade of the P. W. Department allotted to candidates from our engineering colleges. The other ground for discontent among the civil engineers has less foundation in fact. There had, doubtless, been an undue weight given to tact and pleasant manners in selecting men for the secretariat and the Consulting Engineer's branches. On the other hand no dispassionate observer can doubt that these qualities are conspicuous in the products of Woolwich and Chatham. Outside these very small sections there is really no ground to suspect partiality in the authorities for Royal Engineers. The department is divided into several wholly distinct branches—those of Road, and Buildings; Irrigation, and Railways. An officer who has cast his lot in with the first may find that his coevals in other lines have distanced him; and that owing to no fault of his own. But inequalities of promotion must always arise where a profession affords and careers so diverse. It is precisely the same with the regular army. In one regiment a captaincy is reached in eight years: in another a subaltern may pine for sixteen ere reaching the proximate goal of his ambition. The grievances of the civil engineers are, therefore, either incurable or illusory: but where palliation was possible it was secured by Sir Charles Elliott's anxious care for the interests of his subordinates.

CHAPTER VI

ADMINISTRATION OF BENGAL.

In November 1890 Sir Charles Elliott received the offer from Lord Lansdowne of the Lieutenant-Governorship of Bengal, which was about to be vacated by Sir Steuart Bayley. He hesitated long ere he accepted the thorny crown. Difficulties which would have dismayed a less vigorous mind lay before him. Bengal, as he told the guests at a farewell dinner given by the covenanted service to its retiring chief, is second only to Russia in the demand it makes on the administrative faculties of its ruler. He was new to the Province, and unknown to nine-tenths of his future colleagues. How far he has justified the expectations of his friends must be discussed at that date, which Bengal hopes is yet distant, when he shall seek the well-earned repose of private life. We live too near the events which have followed on his accession to power to judge them from the historian's stand point. And then, though we seldom recognize the fact, all human actions are links in a chain of causation stretching through unnumbered ages. The true value, therefore, of isolated facts cannot be appraised until time shall have displayed their ultimate consequences. Our judgment, too,

H

is apt to be distorted by passion or prejudice, disturbing the attitude of calm scrutiny which the historian must adopt if his work is to be aught save a nine days' wonder. "We may blush to think," writes Lord Mahon, "that even those years which, on looking back, are universally admitted most prosperous and those actions now considered irreproachable were not free at the time from most loud and angry complaints. How much has prosperity been felt, but how little acknowledged! How sure a road to popularity has it always been to tell us that we are the most wretched and ill-used people on the face of the earth! To such an extent, in fact, have these outcries proceeded that a very acute observer has founded a new theory on them; and, far from viewing them as evidence of suffering, considers them as one of the proofs and tokens of good government." It is only natural that the policy of an ardent reformer—of one who is not content that a thing should be done well if it can be done better—should excite acrimonious and unreasoning criticism; and that the aspirations which prompt it should be persistently misunderstood. A recapitulation of the chief measures which have characterized Sir Charles Elliott's brief career as Lieutenant-Governor of Bengal, may serve to correct misapprehensions and pave the way for the future annalist.

Among the drawbacks of our executive system, is the fact that offices which make the heaviest demands on the bodily and mental vigour often devolve on men who are long past their prime. Hence the dread of responsibility, the laxity and the want of backbone which have again and again led to disaster during the past decade. No part of India stood in greater need of a reformer than this fair province of Bengal, when, in December 1890, Sir Charles Elliott was called on to guide her destinies. His exhaustless energy and self-reliance led him to take nothing for granted, and to place the most venerable institutions on their trial. This apparent oblivion of the labours of former travellers on well-beaten paths, and of the fact, as true in our day, as in Horace's, that many strong men lived before Agamemnon, is a characteristic perchance better suited to the government of a brand-new colony than of a province where intense conservatism underlies an apparent assimilation of western ideas. But no one who knows him will deny that he has sufficient patience to listen to the views of others and sufficient candour to give them their due weight.

Recognizing the fact that sound finance is the mainspring of good government, Sir Charles Elliott's most strenuous efforts have been directed to increasing the scanty resources which imperial exigencies, real or supposed, place at his disposal.

The quinquennial revision of the financial relations
between the supreme and the provincial governments took place during the current year. The
Lieutenant-Governor seized the opportunity thus
afforded of expressing his views on this point with
no uncertain voice. Full justice was done by the
Government of India to the efficiency with which
the revenues of Bengal had been administered
during the term of the expiring contract. The
income from civil services had expanded from
Rx. 3,410,000 to Rx. 3,610,000; that from railways from Rx. 2,200,000 to Rx. 2,975,000. But
it proposed to sweep a portion of a prospective
increment, which might be as much as Rx. 190,000
annually, into the imperial coffers. The Bengal
Government was deprived of control over the
Tirhut State Railway, and of all income derivable
therefrom : and the project of imperializing that
main source of our provincial revenue—the Eastern Bengal Railway system—was also mooted.
Sir Charles Elliott, who is blessed in an eminent
degree with the courage of his opinions, protested
strongly against any further curtailment of the
revenues. The period to which the contracts were
restricted was, he argued, too short; for the
consequences of good finance or of the reverse
cannot be fully developed in five years. Better
far it would be to declare the whole revenue of
Bengal provincial and levy certain fixed percen-

tages for imperial needs, than make each period
of revision a signal for more exorbitant demands.
The Government of India is nought but a vast
spending department. Incalculable sums are flung
into the abyss of frontier defence : while, owing
to the apathy with which the glaring defects in our
monetary system are regarded, we see the volume
of home charges constantly swelling. Unproduc-
tive expenditure must be controlled with jealous
care ; or in other words, the credit side of the
imperial budget should be stationary, or at least,
slowly progressive. On the other hand there are
no limits to the benefits which would flow from a
policy of real decentralization in finance. Bengal
labours under climatic disadvantages such as no
other tract of the like area endures. Vast systems
of drainage are urgently needed if the central and
eastern districts are to be anything but a hot-bed
of disease. Roads, feeder railway-lines, water-
supply, medical relief—such are a few out of many
pressing wants. All might be supplied in a decade
or two if the government had but the power of
granting adequate assistance by way of loans or
subsidies to local bodies charged with the construction of works of public utility. The same fearless
eagerness to stand up for the right was exempli-
fied in a protest against that fanaticism which
deems the revenues of India and the health of
countless millions as nought compared with a

passion for notoriety and hysterical sentiment. In answer to that baneful influence commonly known as "Exeter Hall" he pointed out that the increase in our revenue for opium consumed in India had been barely eight per cent in ten years—not more than was proportionate to the growth of population in consuming districts. He urged that the closure of licensed shops for the sale of opium would certainly drive men to lose their health and money in illicit dens. He put in a good word for a much-abused and misunderstood drug by asserting, that it enables its votaries to do heavy tasks at a minimum cost of tissue, and is reputed to be a prophylactic of malaria in the steamy swamps of Lower Bengal. Ever eager to develop the resources at his disposal, the Lieutenant-Governor directed that the manufacture of salt by Government agency should be resumed in districts on the Bay of Bengal, where its cost is hardly a sixth of that entailed by the produce of Cheshire. Of equal importance with sound finance is a good judicial and policy system. Here, too, Sir Charles Elliott's ceaseless activity has found a useful outlet. The working of the Calcutta Small Cause Court—an institution corresponding with our English County Courts but vouchsafed larger powers—had been the subject of hostile criticism, due, perhaps, to the fierce light which beats about all forms of governmental agency in the metropolis, rather than to its inherent defects. A close enquiry made it clear that the method of transacting business there compared favourably with that of kindred institutions in Bombay and Madras, except as regards the duration of contested cases. The excessive delays were largely due to a want of method in framing the cause list and too frequent postponements. These have now been reduced by the device of postponing cases not reached or part-heard *de die in diem.* In consonance with the views of the native community Sir Charles Elliott protested against a proposed reduction of the Small Cause Court Judges' jurisdiction from suits of Rx. 200 in value to those of half that amount; and objected to the option of an appeal to the High Court being permitted. He remarked that the arrears would be sensibly lessened by an indulgence in fewer holidays and a lengthening of the hours spent in Court. There can be no doubt that some curtailment is needed in the licence in regard to vacations arrogated by our Civil Courts. It is a survival of the usages imported from England by the old Supreme Court. The re-organization of the subordinate judicial service was a matter of still greater urgency. Yearly swells the volume of litigation; and everywhere a cry rises for more civil courts of the first instance. The intense monotony of life in the interior leads men to give vent to their surplus energies in the arena

offered by the courts of law. An experienced
district judge, who had been employed in enquiries
as to the need of strengthening our judicial staff,
had recommended large additions in the lower
grades. Sir Charles Elliott supported his proposal, observing, however, that newly-founded
Civil Courts rarely paid their way at first; and
that the Supreme Government must expect a
heavy addition to our liabilities for the cost of the
additional establishments. It was only fair, he
argued, that a large proportion of the loss should
be met by a reassignment of provincial revenues.
The administration of criminal justice is still more
closely connected with executive functions. Here
the local knowledge gained by His Honor during
his extended tours stood him in good stead. He
had, too, before him the report of a strong committee appointed by his predecessor to enquire
into the admitted defects of our police system,
which is largely dependent on the working of the
courts. A lack of close supervision on the part
of the district chief; irregularity in attendance at
court on that of his subordinates; frequent and
unnecessary remands—such were a few of the
many defects revealed by these enquiries. They
have been, in large measure, remedied. Deputy
Magistrates now make it a point of honour not to
plead want of time as an excuse for adjourning a
case and a greater degree of zeal has been infus-

ed into all ranks of public servants. The internal organization of the police has not been neglected. Increased pay and allowances have been conceded to the rank and file; and superior educational qualifications insisted on in those which we may call the non-commissioned grades. The reserves have been reorganized, on a military basis; and legislation has been sketched out in view of improving the condition and increasing the powers of that backbone of good district government, the village watchman. Convinced by personal experience of the benefit to the people resulting from frequent tours by heads of departments, Sir Charles Elliott framed a code of rules prescribing a minimum period to be spent in the interior by each officer. The resolution embodying these orders excited considerable comment, and the wisdom of fettering the discretion of high officials was questioned far and wide. It must, however, be admitted, that in this and other respects, Sir Charles's theory and practice coincide. He shuns delights and lives laborious days. No considerations of personal comfort are allowed to outweigh those connected with this primary duty: and few portions indeed of the vast province committed to his care have not been passed in review by him.

The well-being of the agriculturist is of greater importance in Bengal than in any other Presidency. Various causes had conspired to

impair it. The Permanent Settlement left the
immemorial rights of the tenantry at the mercy
of an unscrupulous landlord. The fierce competition for land, resulting from the advance of
population and the ruin of handicrafts by English
competition, had riveted the chains imposed by
Lord Cornwallis and his advisers. The first really
successful attempt to protect the tiller of the soil
was made in the much abused Tenancy Act of
1885. One of the most important clauses in this,
the ryots' Magna Charta, renders it possible for
the authorities to insist on a survey and record of
rights being carried out in any tract which had
not been subjected to these processes. The
necessity of putting this law in force is felt more
or less in every district ; but nowhere more press-
ingly than in Northern Behar, where rack-renting
and extortion of all kinds leave the unhappy ryot
within a hair's breadth of famine. Sir Charles
Elliott pleaded the cause of these really dumb
millions. He pointed out that a cadastral survey
was merely an importation of accurate methods
and skilled supervision into a process which all
Zemindars are forced by self-interest to attempt
for themselves. The proposed survey was therefore, in a good landlord's interest : for it would enable him to recover large tracts which carelessness
and rule-of-thumb have left in the possession of
squatters. The ryots on the other hand, would

secure a bulwark against invasion of their rights
by village tyrants. Who shall say that these
advantages are dearly bought at an expenditure
of seven annas—hardly as many pence—per acre ?
His Honor admitted frankly that furious and
obstinate opposition would be excited by the
survey. Ignorance would conspire with an interest in maintaining the countless abuses arising
from the existing chaos to prejudice mens' minds
against a most useful reform. Sir Charles Elliott,
however, argued that the results would be well
worth the cost : and urged that a cadastral survey
of 12,500 square miles in North Behar, to be
completed in five years, might receive the sanction of the Viceroy and Secretary of State.
These high functionaries acceded this warm support to the proposal ; and in spite of keen opposition the great measure has been definitely resolved
on.

His Honor is, indeed, the last man to shrink
from personal odium when it is entailed by a
course dictated by his sense of duty. Nowhere
is the need for sanitation more pronounced than
in our most advanced Province ; and nowhere,
alas, is it less understood and recognized. The
public bodies which are the fruits of Lord Ripon's
policy of Self-Government, have not invariably
risen to the occasion. Our towns are hotbeds of
disease. Sir Charles was forced to admit that

the well-meant attempt to associate the people in the management of public affairs was half a century in advance of the times we live in. While the power of municipalities must be enlarged, the bonds uniting them with the authority of Government officers stand in equal need of strengthening. The Sanitary Commissioner had been little else than a quasi-ornamental appendage of Government. He has been developed into a Sanitary Board with greatly enlarged powers, and special engineering experience at his call. The Vaccination Department too has undergone drastic reform. Centralization had been pushed to external limits, and no pains had been taken to gain the help and countenance of local officials. All this is now changed. The district is now the unit in vaccine operations. Civil Surgeons, who are posted at each head quarters, are responsible for work within their several charges, and a strong staff of inspectors and sub-inspectors have been placed under their supervision. Education in the true sense of the word must precede the attempt to enforce sanitary rules. Sir Charles Elliott has given free scope to his predecessor Sir George Campbell's far-seeing policy which dotted the provinces with primary schools. Municipalities are enjoined to devote a larger share of their revenues to the support of such. That which is called high education is too firmly established to need state bolstering. The District High Schools will, therefore, be surrendered to the care of local bodies. The too long neglected cause of technical education has received his earnest support. Amongst his reform has been an entire re-casting of the Engineering College at Sibpur. It occupies the site selected by that gentle enthusiast Bishop Heber for the cherished foundation by the aid of which he hoped to bring the best traditions of our English Universities to bear on the training of young converts for the Christian Ministry. His Honor declared that the increase in the number of youths educated for engineering pursuits and qualified to develop the resources of the province was an object on which he was justified in incurring a large outlay, inasmuch as he was confident that all such outlay would be fully reproductive. The College now consists of an Engineering section and one devoted to the technical training of apprentices. Four appointments in the upper subordinate grades of the Department of Public Works are now filled by competition amongst its pupils. The College examination, with two years' practical training, is accepted as qualifying for the post of Engineer under the District Boards. The technical schools which those bodies are forming throughout the interior will, in time be affiliated with Sibpur. We are, in fact, in a fair way of seeing the reproach removed

that English rule has done little towards reviving
the technical skill for which India was once world-
renowned, but which has been crushed beneath
the heel of Western competition.

The tribes on our eastern frontier have made
themselves unpleasantly conspicuous of late.
Nowhere are civilization and utter barbarism in
closer contact than in the rich tracts bordering
on the habitat of the fierce Lushais. This country
has lately been made a separate administrative
change ; and the task of overawing them facilitated
by a very large expenditure on roads and bridges.

Nor amid the care and drudgery of his high
office has the cause of charity and social progress
been neglected by Sir Charles Elliott. He is a
warm supporter of that movement for bringing
skilled medical and surgical aid home to the helpless
women of this country which will illustrate Lady
Dufferin's name when the political and diplomatic
triumphs of her husband shall have passed into
oblivion. The Fund owes to him a donation of
Rs. 15,000, which should serve as a stimulus to
the generosity of others who have far fewer claims
on their purses than a Lieutenant-Governor of
Bengal. There is, indeed no movement which
aims at lessening the sorrows of life or increasing
its innocent pleasures which does not find in him
a warm supporter. The task thus imposed would
be beyond his strength but for the active sympa-

thy of Lady Elliott, who nobly seconds his efforts
for the common good.

This imperfect sketch of a great and useful
career speaks a moral which he that runs may
read.   High aims persistently followed lead to
honour and renown, and, that which is sweeter
still to noble minds, they bring with them the consciousness of talents well applied, of evil impulses
eradicated, of good instincts fostered and streng-
thened.   Of Sir Charles Elliott may be said that
which John Stuart Mill proudly records of his
father, the historian of British India :—

" His moral inculcations were at all times,
those of the *Socratici Viri*—justice, temperance
(to which he gave a very extended application),
veracity, perseverance, readiness to encounter pain,
and especially labour, regard for the public good ;
the estimation of persons according to their merits
and things according to their instrinsic usefulness ;
a life of exertion in contradistinction to one of
self-indulgent ease and sloth."

APPENDIX

CONTAINING SELECTED PUBLIC ADDRESSES BY SIR CHARLES
ELLIOTT AS LIEUTENANT-GOVERNOR.

◆

SPEECH ON THE INAUGURATION OF THE DUF-FERIN HOSPITAL, CALCUTTA, 2ND MARCH, 1891.

His Honor the Lieutenant-Governor, in inviting her
Excellency to declare the hospital open, said :—Your Excellency,—The report which you have heard read contains so
full an account of the history and objects of this institution
that very few words, in addition, are needed from me on this
occasion, for all of you, ladies and gentlemen, have had or
will now have an opportunity of inspecting the building, and
you will, I am sure, feel satisfied that it has been well and
sagaciously planned, that the accommodation provided is moderate in quantity and suitable in quality, and that we have good
reason for hoping that it will soon be in full working order,
and that the classes for whose benefit it is designed will flock
to it and will obtain relief from much physical suffering
through its aid. It is a great cause for satisfaction that your
Excellency is not opening to-day only the portion of the main
building, the construction of which is finished, but that you
are really opening the whole set of subsidiary buildings which
the original planners of the institution designed. A hospital
such as we see before us would be altogether unsuitable and
inadequate without the addition of a dispensary and a con-
sulting-room for out-patients, quarters for the resident doctor
and matron, separate accommodation for wealthier patients and
out offices. All of these, I rejoice to say, have now been
provided. The offer of the money required for a children's
ward has been nobly answered, and I have the great pleasure
of announcing that the whole of the sum required to meet it

•

had been subscribed by yesterday. The list of subscribers whose names have been received since the report was printed is as follows :—

Raja Janki Bulluv Sen, of Rungpur	4,000
Nawab Bahadur of Moorshidabad	1,000
Raja Govind Lall Ray, of Rungpur	1,000
Rai Dhunput Singh Bahadur	1,000
Babu Hem Chunder Gossain, of Serampur	500
Sir Andrew Scoble	500
Fakhiroonnisa Begum, of Gya	200
Nawab Syed Zaimul Abideen Khan Bahadoor, Teroze Jung of Moorshidabad	130
Prince Jehan Kudr (2nd donation)	125
Syed Ameer Hossein	100
Syed Ali Belgrami, of Hyderabad	100
Syed Ikbul Ali Khan, Bahadur of Hyderabad	100
Kajah Wahid Jan of Gya	100
Mr. Meugens	500
Babu Janokey Nath Roy	1,000

In addition to this, Nawab Ashanoollah Khan Bahadur, of Dacca, has intimated that he will make up any balance required. I am proud to think that Bengal has nobly responded to the call I made upon her, and that the reproaches which were levelled at her at the last annual meeting have been wiped away and cannot again be repeated (Applause). But while I mention these contributions with pride and pleasure, I would not have it forgotten that there are other contributions more valuable than money. You all remember the lines of Tennyson :—

> I asked them, give me immortality,
> Then didst thou part in asking with a smile,
> Like wealthy men who care not how they give.

I do not undervalue the gifts of money, for we cannot do without them, but I cannot forget that many persons may appear liberal who do not deny themselves one pleasure or

luxury, or suffer one moment's inconvenience in consequence
of these gifts. I do emphatically say that the hard-worked
official or business man who out of his scanty leisure contri-
butes time and thought to the furtherance of a scheme like
this does more real service to the cause than many whose
money contributions are blazoned abroad. Service of this
sort has been freely rendered by Mr. Guyther, the Executive
Engineer, who not only prepared the plans, but also super-
vised the whole work of construction; the names of other
members of the P. W. D., who have worked with and under
him with equal alacrity have been mentioned by the Honorary
Secretary. It is a great pleasure to me to be able to record
these good works on the part of the Department with which
I was lately so exclusively connected. But the most important assistance of all of this kind has been contributed by Mr.
Cotton (Applause), the indefatigable Secretary of the Bengal
Branch of the Dufferin Fund. Those who know how heavily
and continuous a Secretary's work is will best be able to
realize the greatness of the service which Mr. Cotton has
rendered to the cause by the large amount of voluntary work
which he has undertaken and ably carried out in its behalf.
Last, but not least, I may be permitted to say that you, Lady
Lansdowne, are included in the list of benefactors of this
class, both for the constant and assiduous labour you have
undertaken as President of the Dufferin Fund, and also in
that you have graciously consented, in spite of the burdens
of your many public engagements, to favour us by your
presence at this ceremony—a condescension for which, on
behalf of all present, I have to tender you our sincere thanks.
(Applause.) And now I will conclude with a prayer in which
I am sure that all the people assembled here, whether Chris-
tians or Jews, Mahomedans or Hindus, will join—that the
blessing of Almighty God may rest upon this undertaking,
and that the Dufferin Hospital in Calcutta may fulfil all that
we expect of it, and may be the means of rescuing many of

the women and children of this great city from physical
suffering and premature death. (Loud applause.) I ask your
Excellency to declare the Hospital open.

SPEECH ON THE INAUGURATION OF
THE VICTORIA HALL, HUGHLI, JULY 11TH, 1891.

His Honor in reply said that he had responded with much
pleasure to the invitation to declare the Victoria Hall open,
because, independently of the great gratification it was to him
to visit Hughli and make the acquaintance of the large, and
highly-educated community of the town, it was especially
interesting owing to his always having heard of Hughly as
being less peculiarly Indian than most other places. Long
before coming to Bengal he had more than once discussed
with Bengal officers the respective merits of the Patriarchal
system of Government as practised in the North Western
Provinces and Upper India, where his own training had been,
and of the more legal and more elaborately organized system
of Government through or with the help of local bodies and
the leaders of Native society. In these discussions Hughli
had always been held up as a district in which the inhabitants
were so educated, so loyal, and so sensible of the true requirements of the administration and of the assistance that can be
given by local self-government that that district at least could
do without the Patriarchal system. He now met for the first
time the assembled community, and so far as he could judge
from appearances this report of Hughli was true. The objects
of Government seemed to be understood, its views supported
by the good sense of the people, and they were ever ready to
assist the local administration. The fact of their building
the hall in which they were assembled in commemoration of
the Jubilee of their gracious Sovereign and naming it after
her showed the loyalty and good feeling that actuated their
lives.

His Honor wished to lay particular stress at this particular time on this point, for just now there was a wave of
disloyalty and distrust abroad the origin of which sprang from
a certain Bill introduced at the commencement of the year.
He wished to appeal to the good sense of such a community
as that assembled to do their best to put down such sentiments. Political disputes must of necessity always have in
their train feelings of bitterness; but it behoved all good
citizens to abstain from prolonged agitation and to bury the
hatchet as soon as possible, and also to discourage those who
try to stir up a spirit of race-hatred and alienation. The
good intentions of the Government should be accepted and
not only should bygones be bygones, but it was through the
loyalty of the upper and better educated classes that better
feeling should be revived. Here in Hughli, he might just
mention one particular opportunity of assisting Government
and showing good feeling. It had been brought to his notice
that a Hindu gentleman was in the habit of causing annoyance
to his Mahomedan neighbours in the Imambara by beating
gongs and blowing trumpets during their hours of prayer.
Now nobody was entitled and nobody who was at all enlightened would wish, to exercise his own religious feelings
in such a way as to hurt the religious feelings of others. Every
man of right feeling ought to allow to others the same religious
toleration and respect which he would wish for himself. His
Honor said he was glad to think that so far as he could judge,
his words seemed to meet with approval, and he trusted that
the good sense of the community would settle matters ami-
cably, and that he should not hear of any necessity arising for
the intervention of the Magistrate and the employment of the
police in this matter, but that Hughli would maintain its fair-fame
as an enlightened and well ordered town. His Honor then
said that he would reply to the points mentioned in the address.

First as regards drainage. He had no definite information
which was with him as regards the scheme, but he understood

that such a scheme had been prepared and it would be called for. If it appeared to be good and sufficient then he would assist by sanctioning a Government loan on easy terms, as had been done in the cases of Howrah, Utterpara, &c., under the conditions laid down by the Supreme Government.

The second point was the water-supply. This was one he had very much at heart. There were at present two schemes before the Sanitary Board for the supply of water to riparian Municipalities. The first was that works were to be established opposite and similar to those of Fulta for the supply of all riparian Municipalities on the right bank. This seemed the better scheme in some ways, but the chief difficulty would be the allotment of fair proportion of expenses to the several riparian Municipalities. The second scheme was that each Municipality should have its own pumping, settling, and filtering machinery for its own supply, and this would be cheaper in some respects, as for instance in necessitating a much less length of piping; but the cost of machinery and working would probably be much greater. Whatever the scheme might be, however, he expressed a hearty desire to see during his term of office a supply of good water to all riparian Municipalities. As regards railway stations by the Hughly Bridge the question had been brought forward once before, and should be again enquired into, as it was possible that local wishes might, at any rate, be met so far as the establishment of a narrow passenger platform was concerned.

SPEECH ON THE PRESENTATION OF ADDRESSES AT MYMENSINGH.

His Honor the Lieutenant-Governor replying thanked the representatives of the several Associations for their very friendly and loyal welcome, and expressed his gratitude for the kind expressions contained in each and all. He was glad to see that they had not only noticed, but had also been satisfied with the efforts of the Government of Bengal since he had the honor of being at its head, and assured them that Government's greatest desire was to devote itself to watching over their welfare. He has long wished to visit this large and important centre, Mymensingh; and it had been one of his first cares to select a special Magistrate and Collector for so heavy a charge. In Mr. Phillips the District possessed an officer of the highest ability and of indefatigable energy, and it was to be hoped that his health would permit of his remaining long enough to carry through the many important works of the District. As regards the address of the District Board, it was one of unusual importance, owing to the very wide view it took of the requirements of the district, and his Honor said he could not do more than touch on some of the points alluded to, and leave the others to be treated in the secretariat, for which he would, however, issue special orders. In referring to the Municipal Address, his Honor expressed his sympathy with the members of the Committee in their loss of so able a Chairman, but trusted his successor would prove himself to be equally capable. The address contained a request that the ferry revenues might be handed over for certain purposes, and he hoped before leaving the town to be able to make a personal inspection, and if the projects seemed in every way desirable the request should be granted. In reply to the address from the Mahomedan Association his Honor assured the members that he had always sympathised with their wants, and that Government were equally willing and anxious to give them their fair share in all appointments, but it was absolutely necessary that they would fit themselves for the posts. Though Government was bound to divide its patronage as fairly as possible, it was an equally sacred duty that only those qualified for appointments should hold them, and it was a regrettable fact that great difficulty was experienced in finding qualified Mahomedan candidates. The remarks about local schools seemed reasonable, and the District Board would be asked to give the matter their consideration and what help and encouragements they could. The re-establishment of the Madrassa was a question that had not yet been brought to notice, and his Honor could not therefore give any sort of reply, except that it would be referred to Sir Alfred Croft for report, who, no doubt, would gladly embrace the opportunity of assisting the Mahomedans as far as he could; and as far as was fair he, no doubt, would help with a share of the Government funds. In reply to the gentlemen of Sherpur his Honor said he hoped on some future occasion to be able to visit them in their own homes, and see something of their villages, but though the Magistrate had kindly arranged that he should drive out and see one or two of the Sherpur gentlemen, the plan had unfortunately been abandoned owing to want of time. The request they made for a railway was already included in the scheme proposed by the District Board, which went a very great deal further, and was a very large request, indeed, even for an extensive district like this. It was very simple for a district to make such requests, but were each to do so the sum total would be something appalling. The project of the District Board would require at least some 50 lakhs, which was out of the question, but a survey of the Tangail line should be made. It had always to be remembered that in dealing with funds for railways the funds were Imperial and not Provincial, and that there was only a certain sum available each year. Of this Bengal, of course, got its share, and were it possible to do so a loan of the necessary eight lakhs or so would be lent for the counstruction of this line on the security of the District Board. The continuation of the line to Sherpur would be a very much more difficult concern, owing to its involving the construction of a great length of bridge, which would be quite beyond the means of the Provincial Government. The funds, therefore, would have to be asked for from the Imperial coffers, and not only would be a very clear case of necessity for the line have to be made out,

but also a very decided prospect of profit. Even so it was highly
improbable that Government would grant the necessary sanction and funds, considering that such great projects as the
Assam-Chittagong line, which for years had been a pet scheme,
were as yet unfinished, and would require several crores for
completion. Government only had a certain sum annually
for such works, in which a great hole would be made were
they to grant six lakhs here and eight lakhs there for small
local requirements. His Honor then expressed his satisfaction
at hearing of the construction and maintenance of roads, founding of scholarships, and other such good works, which were
a distinct step in advance; and on behalf of the Government
he thanked those gentlemen who were expending their time
and energy on behalf of their countrymen. His Honor then
said that after all these sentiments of approval he was bound to
add a word of disagreement, and that was because he was
sorry to find the address of the District Board penetrated by
the idea so common in this country, that the people should
look entirely to Government for support, or, as they put it
in the address, State nursing, State aid, and State subsidies.
It was absolutely necessary in these days of enlightenment and
progress that they should learn to stand alone, and alone
to work out their own requirements. The Government of
India had already as much to do as it could manage and it
was a well-known fact that its officials were overworked. The
difficulty about the looseness of the nuptial tie among the lower
classes of Mahomedans was a great misfortune, but it was not
for law to step in where morality was concerned; for what was
the good of law where the public conscience did not carry it
out? A time no doubt would come when education and
civilization would work the necessary remedy. As regards
the request for a Mahomedan Marriage Registration Act,
his Honor said he was by no means in favor of it, and would
certainly never bring forward such a Bill until a great majority
of the Mahomedans had requested him to do so, and at

present he believed there was a very decided feeling against it. In conclusion, his Honor explained at considerable length how wrong both in theory and practice was the State aid for which people were so ready to ask.

REPLY TO AN ADDRESS OF THE INDIGO PLANTERS OF BEHAR AND SONEPUR, NOV., 1891.

His Honor, replying, said to Mr. Hudson and the gentlemen representing the Indigo Planters' Association, that he had received with great satisfaction the address with which they had been good enough to welcome him on his arrival among them in Behar, and that he very cordially reciprocated these kind feelings, and hoped that his arrival among them would leave nothing but present recollections both in their minds and in his own. Coming among them as he did, almost a complete stanger to Behar, they would not, of course, expect him to say much about the details of their work. He came more with the object of learning the position of the Indigo industry than for the purpose of giving any opinion on the subject, and he trusted that he would have the opportunity of gaining much knowledge that would be useful to himself. What he knew at present about the industry was to a large extent due to a report drawn up by his predecessor Sir Stewart Bayley just before resigning office. This report had lately been published as a Parliamentary paper, and he would read to them a few passages in order to give publicity to those views : Sir Ashley Eden, addressing the Indigo Planters' Association, said :—"I take this opportunity of thanking your Association for the cordial co-operation which you have always given to me and the officers of Government, for the admirable influence which you have exercised throughout Behar and for the conciliatory and moderate spirit in which you have adjusted disputes between contending interests." He then read extracts from the Administration Report of the Patna

Division for the year 1883-84. The Commissioners wrote as follows:—"With regard to the Behar Indigo Planters' Association, I understand that it is doing much good work. The Secretary of the Association complains that some indigo planters benefit by the institution while declining to be bound by its rules or to contribute to its necessary expenses. He thinks that an expression of opinion on the part of the Government would be sufficient to induce these gentlemen to join the Association." Sir Charles was sorry to find that this anticipation of the Commissioner had not altogether been realized. Another report says:—"The Secretary of the Behar Indigo Planters' Association writes to the Collector of Mozufferpore that he believes the relations between planters, zemindars, and ryots are satisfactory, and that during the past year there has been hardly any necessity for the interference of the Association with the affairs of any factory." He adds: "The operations of the Cadastral Survey Department under Colonel Barrow, and of the record of rights under Mr. Collin were begun in November last, and there has been, I am happy to believe, no friction between the members of the Association and the officers mentioned, owing in a great measure to the tact and courtesy displayed by them in all matters which have been brought to their notice." Another report says:—"The Indigo Planters' Association furnishes the best possible instance of local self-government. It is completely voluntary. It is latent till occasion arises, and then it springs into action." And the last passage in that part of the report, that dealt with Behar and which sums up Sir S. C. Bayley's own views, were as follows:—"A reference to the general correspondence of this Government shows that whereas formerly the object of indigo was a burning one, which gave constant anxiety and required unremitted attention, it now really elicits allusions such as those quoted from the Administration Report—a change which indicates how much more smoothly the work is carried on at present." He needed hardly to say to the gentlemen there present that he had read these reports with great satisfaction, and he trusted that the opinion formed by such experienced men were still justified, and that the working of their Association was still directed to smoothing away and removing all harshness and injustice, and that the members were doing all in their power to ensure the progress and success of this great industry.

One passage which he had just read spoke of the experimental cadastral survey carried on in the Mozufferpur district about four years ago. He would take this opportunity of referring especially to that, because, as they no doubt were aware, the cadastral survey was about to be commenced in the four districts of Northern Behar. He need hardly say that he had not entered on an undertaking of this kind without a due sense of the difficulties that might arise and the considerable labour that it would entail on himself and many of his officers. It was not a work one would undertake with a light heart. He knew that there had already been signs of an agitation commencing against it, but he was quite satisfied that the cadastral survey was wanted in this country, and that it would be highly beneficial. From what he had been able to learn from some of their number, he believed that all the most influential members would welcome the measure. It would give them an accurate knowledge of every one's rights with which they had to deal. They were all of them obliged to have constant dealings both with ryots and landholders, and it would be found to be most important to know the exact extent of those rights conferred upon them by the Tenancy Act. The third great class interested in the question was the Zemindars, and from them he knew that some agitation and opposition might be expected, but he hoped that these would melt away when they heard more of the facts. Every Zemindar was obliged to keep up a record of his ryots, their holdings, and their rents, but this record was generally most inaccurate, as for the most part they were obliged to rely on the Patwari who was not described as a trustworthy person. Well, the survey would give them an accurate record of these facts, and would clear up all the disputes and uncertainties which caused so much annoyance and loss. He trusted it was hardly necessary for him to assure the Zemindars that Government would not have entered on this undertaking unless it had been convinced that it would be for the good and not the harm of the landlords. He was convinced that when the three parties most interested, the ryots, the zemindars, and planters, came to know what the Survey really meant, they would welcome it as a thing beneficial to themselves.

He had just issued a Resolution, which he hoped they would read carefully when it was published in the next Government *Gazette* and the newspapers, and he gladly took this opportunity of explaining its contents and arguments briefly to them. He trusted that all who read it and understood its full scope and intentions would lend him their hearty co-operation in the performance of this arduous task. The Indigo Planters' Association had been spoken of as a part of the Administrative Machine, assisting Government and being in return assisted by Government. As long as they carried out this silent compact which was made with them by Sir Ashley Eden, and carried on their operations with justice and equity, he could assure them that the Association would receive his hearty support. In conclusion, he begged to thank them cordially for the kind way in which they had received him, and he would look forward to the remainder of his tour as likely to be equally pleasant and profitable to him as it had hitherto been.

SPEECH ON THE DUFFERIN FUND.

The following Address was delivered at a meeting of the supporters of the Countess of Dufferin's Fund. H. E. the Viceroy in the Chair, Jan. 1892.

The best manner in which we can show our thanks to your Excellencies for the support and encouragement of this

Society, is by showing what has been done by it or for it during the past year, what progress we have made, and what we hope to make. We have now five female hospitals in Bengal, in Calcutta, in Bhagulpore, Durbhanga, Gya and Cuttack, and at all of these, with one exception, the number of patients who have received medical attendance was larger than in the preceding year. The one exception, I am sorry to say, is that of the Dufferin Hospital in Calcutta; there, though the in-patients increased from 118 to 173, the number of out-door patients fell from 21,000 to about 17,000. There were, we believe, two reasons for this; one was the death of Mrs. Foggo who had become well known, and had gained the confidence of the public, and it was not unnatural that it would take a little time for her successor to acquire a similar following, and that the numbers should fall off for a time. The other reason was that the Eden Hospital had opened a dispensary for women coming as out-door patients, and this had, of course, tended to compete with the Dufferin Hospital, but so far as this cause operates it is satisfactory to know that more medical care, not less, is being bestowed on women. We have good reason to hope that the results will tend to a larger attendance at both institutions next year. Besides these we have no less than four hospitals which are well on their way to existence. That at Bettiah of which Lady Elliott lately laid the foundation stone, we owe to the munificence of the Maharajah of Bettiah. The brother of the Maharajah of Durbhanga, Raja Rameswar Singh Bahadoor has undertaken to provide funds for starting a women's hospital at Raj Nagar, and though the project has not advanced during the year, I have no doubt that he will perform his promise at an early date. While I was in Behar I received a very generous donation from a mahomedan gentleman of the place of Rs 10,000 towards founding a hospital in Patna, and another Indian gentleman has privately undertaken to supply whatever funds are requisite to complete and start the building, so that I may congratulate Patna, the second town in Bengal, on the prospect that this want will shortly be satisfied. Within the last few days I have heard of the Collection of Funds for a hospital at Dinajpur, and I hope that this institution will soon be started. This is certainly a good tale of progress for a single year as regards the creation of women's hospitals.

Next, as to the number of ladies of different degrees of skill and training, who are employed under the Dufferin Fund in the treatment of women, our report is as follows : We have one lady Doctor of the first class, who is in charge of the Dufferin Hospital, Calcutta; of the second grade, those who have taken the degree of Licentiates in medicine and surgery, we have five at Bhagalpur, Darbhanga, Gya, Cuttack and Chittagong; of the third grade, who correspond to hospital assistants, we have only three, at Murshidabad, Burdwan and Kamarhatti. In order to test how we stand in this respect, it is well to compare ourselves with our sister province of the North-West, the province in which this Society has received its widest expansion, in so much that of the half million patients of whom you have heard as recipients of medical relief during the past year, about half belong to the North-Western Provinces alone. Well, I find that in the North-West Provinces they have one lady doctor of the first grade—the same number as we have; they have six of the second grade against our five; it is only in the third grade that they are much ahead of us, having, I think, twelve or fifteen against our three. It is clearly necessary for us to do all we can to diminish this difference and to increase the number of our trained and skilled lady doctors. This is, as Mr. Beverley and Mr. Chentral Rao have already told you, the very root of the matter for the Dufferin Society, and if we overcome this difficulty, we may rely on overcoming every other obstacle that stands in our way; but it is a very real difficulty. We have two excellent institutions at which these ladies are trained. At the Medical College, there are 21 female students, but Dr. Birch has not arranged his figures so as to show how many of these are likely to pass out in the next or the following year.   Here the education is of the highest class, and every effort should be strained to keep up the numbers of these students.   At the Campbell Medical School the education only fits the students for the third or hospital assistant grade ; but this is the grade of which as I have shewn, it is most important to increase the numbers. Last year 10 or 11 young women passed out, and when I last visited the school, Dr. Coull-Mackenzie told me that all of these, except, I think, one, had obtained employment, and that one has, I believe, received an appointment since then.   But in the year that is now passing out there is a lamentable falling off—the number is only four, so that we have a very small reserve on which to fall back for filling the new extensions we hope to make.   I trust this decrease is only temporary and accidental, as the numbers in the two lower years are considerably larger, but I strongly feel that this is the direction in which personal effort is most needed.   I would urge this on the influential gentlemen whom I see assembled here. Many of you have large numbers of dependents, often hereditary followers, and if you can impress on them how desirable a thing it is for their girls to take up this new opening in life and to embrace the study of medicine; how useful they will be to their country-women as well as how profitable the profession will be to themselves, you will do more for the spread and success of the Dufferin Society than were if you made the most munificent contributions in money.   Mr. Chentral Rao spoke of stirring up the District Boards and Municipalities to help in this way.   I am glad to say that they have shewn great readiness to do it.   A very large number of the Boards and Municipalities have offered scholarships ; but in too many cases no one has come forward to accept the offer.   I am confident, however, that we need not despond and that is only a question of time before public opinion becomes permeated without object, and expresses itself distinctly on our side.   I have kept

for the last part of my speech the important question of
finance : and the remarks I have to make on this subject are
not so much intended for the present audience, which has the
printed report before it, but I make them in the hope that they
will be fully reported in the newspapers both English and Vernacular, and will penetrate to the mofussil districts, as my
main object is to shew in what way I wish the Provincial
Branch to work, not for Calcutta alone, but for the mofussil.
It is with pride and pleasure that I announce that Bengal has
responded to the appeal which I ventured to make in this hall
last year in a way which has surpassed my most sanguine anti-
cipations. We have received this year Rs. 37,400 for the Building Fund of the Dufferin Hospital, and that project is now
in a secure position, and its extensions are almost completed ;
and we have raised Rs. 32,919, or say, Rs. 33,000 for the General Fund. You will say it is most unreasonable if I am not
altogether satisfied ; and indeed I am fully satisfied with the
amount collected, but not so much so with the composition of
the item. When we put aside sums that are ear-marked, like
the Rs. 10,000 given by my Mahomedan friend at Patna for the
women's hospital, or munificent gifts like the Rs. 10,000 of Mr.
Walter Thomson of Behea and the Rs. 5,000 of the Raja of
Khaira, which we cannot expect to be constantly repeated,
there remains only Rs 8,000 contributed by the general public.
Our expenditure, on the other hand, has been Rs. 14,000 this year,
and this is the normal and recurrent outlay on the Dufferin
Hospital and the Surnomoyi Hospital, which I do not see any
means of largely reducing. One item, indeed, there is which
might be reduced ; and I make a special point of mentioning
it, as I see the Chairman of the Calcutta Corporation present.
Last year it was remarked in more than one quarter that the
Rs. 1,200 per annum subscribed by the Corporation to the
Dufferin Hospital was, if not illiberal, at least not bounteous ;
but they have not thought fit to increase the figure. There,
however, is a charge of Rs. 881 for municipal taxes on the

2   •

Hospital Building; and this is a charge from which I really think they might find it in their hearts to exempt so deserving a charity. I appeal to the Chairman and to any of the Municipal Commissioners who may be present to take this matter into consideration at an early meeting.

Now to resume. Our obligatory expenditure is, as I said, about Rs. 14,000 a year and I want to place that on a firm basis. We receive about Rs. 5,000 a year from our invested funds, and the balance, or Rs. 9,000, is an amount which I make no doubt will be contributed year after year by public charity. I should be very ungrateful for what has been done and very wanting in reasonable confidence for the future if I felt any want of security on this subject.

Even this very day I have received from two generous residents of Calcutta, Messrs. Heera Lal Johory and Gulal Chand a contribution of Rs. 1,500 towards the funds of our Society. But what I am extremely desirous to see are these sums distributed over a wider basis and contributed not in large gifts by a few wealthy persons, but in small amounts by a great number of the well-to-do middle class. This year for the first time, the Provincial Branch is able to announce that it has received a promise of annual subscriptions of Rs. 350 from 14 different people, and many of these subscriptions are in amounts of Rs. 10 and Rs. 12. This is what I want to secure, and what I asked for—not subscriptions of Rs. 50 and Rs. 100 but of Rs. 10 and Rs. 17 and Rs. 20 per annum. It is a great mistake, and a very common Anglo-Indian mistake, to think that a subscription, if given at all, must be a handsome one of Rs. 100 or Rs. 50; the result is that many abstain from giving, and those who give or obliged to give to a more restricted number of charities than they would. I trust that we may receive this year a large influx of small annual sums, the promise of which will afford security of a broad and permanent basis to this charity, and will justify us in carrying out the extensions we aim at.

This brings me to the last point in my speech which is this: say, that we get a permanent income from subscriptions of Rs. 20,000 or Rs. 25,000, what do we intend to do with it? Hitherto our energies have been absorbed in starting the Dufferin Hospital in Calcutta, but it is obvious that we must not be content to remain in this position. It is the mofussil from which, to a large extent, we receive subcriptions, and it is in the mofussil, which needs medical skill and attendance far more than Calcutta with its magnificent provision of hospitals and its abundance of doctors, that our funds should chiefly be spent. The scheme which I intend to propose to the Local Committee is that we should offer to pay half the salary of a medical lady, up to, say, Rs. 30, in every district, and should offer to pay half the cost of erecting a women's ward, up to, say, Rs. 1,000, attached to the hospital at the Head quarters of every district. When I said women's ward I used the wrong word. It is not a ward that I contemplate, but a row of separate rooms suited to the secluded habits of respectable women. We have made a great mistake hitherto in several cases in Bengal by creating wards for women on the same pattern as wards for men. No women but the very poorest will be content to lie in beds six or eight or ten together in a single ward. We must provide separate quarters for them in which they can retain their privacy, and can be visited and attended by their relatives, and I am glad the Maharajah of Bettiah's Hospital is being constructed on this plan. It need not be an expensive plan: indeed, it should be a less costly one than the construction of wards on the usual system. In this way I hope that in a few years, possibly even before I leave this country, I may see a trained lady doctor and a suitable women's Branch Hospital in every district of Bengal. This is the scheme of co-operation with the mofussil which I hope the Provincial Branch will be able to adopt, and this is the prospect of extension of the objects of the society which, I trust, we shall be able to hold out to our friends and supporters in the country. When we have accomplished it we shall have given the truest and most practical expression of our thanks to your Excellency and Lady Lansdowne for the support and encouragement you have given to this most valuable charity. We shall then be able to look this charming portrait of the Marchioness of Dufferin and Ava in the face and say: "We have realized your beneficent aspirations, and the ball which you set rolling we have kept up and carried on to the goal which you aimed at."

REPLY TO ADDRESSES AT BHAGALPUR,
APRIL, 1892.

His Honor said he begged to thank the assembled gentlemen for the very kind and hearty manner in which, in the addresses just read, they had welcomed him on this his first arrival in the town of Bhagalpur, and he wished to assure them how sensible he was of the feelings of loyalty and kindliness which had animated their addresses. He wished to take this opportunity of expressing how much he regretted the unforeseen accident of the previous night, by which they had been caused the inconvenience of such a prolonged detention at the railway station. Had there been any expectation of such a possiblity, he would most certainly have telegraphed, asking that no one might await his arrival. In three out of four addresses reference had been made to the principal object of the present tour, which was, too, the principal thought in the minds of most people, and certainly of all those who were in any way connected with land—the prospect of scarcity and famine in this district. He was, therefore, very glad to be able to reassure his hearers that he did not consider the present state one necessitating alarm. He had visited a considerable portion of the affected parts of the district and a large number of the relief works, and had not seen half-a-dozen persons, all told, who appeared to be suffering from hunger, or who were to any degree emaciated. The present stage appeared to be this, that there is food in the country, and not at excessively high prices, but the ordinary sources of agricultural employment for landless labourers have closed up, and they are no longer able to earn wages by working in the fields as the landlords and ryots alike are unable to pay wages. These classes have, therefore, to work on relief works in order to obtain money to buy food, and the present problem is how to provide a suitable and sufficient programme of such works. Most effectual measures had been taken by Mr. Wace, the Collector, to provide ample labour in all places where the people could possibly require it. Those works which had been started were being carried out in a most reasonable and sagacious manner, and His Honor wished to congratulate the district on their good fortune in having such a Collector at such a time—a man of such ability and sound judgment, as to know exactly how far to start these relief works or where to limit or close them, and yet avoid any possible harshness or severity. It was a most difficult thing to decide the exact time when works should be lessened or extended; and the district was, indeed, fortunate in having in Mr. Wace an officer of both ability, earnestness, and previous experience of famine work.

His Honor said it afforded him great pleasure to be able to announce that the Maharaja of Sonburs á, with his well-known generosity, had offered to Government Rs. 10,000 to be expended on relief works on a road or any other work of utility in the distressed tracts. Babu Janordhan Singh of Barail had offered Rs. 900 for gratuitous relief in Supul. Rani Sitabati offered Rs. 1,000 for the relief of widows and women who could not appear in public. He understood that the Raja of Barwari intended making an offer, of which no doubt he would soon make known the details. The Raja of Baneli and Kumar Nityanand Singh had intimated their intention of jointly undertaking some improvements on their estates, which would serve as relief works, and cost Rs. 7,200. Babu Ganpat Singh intended starting some similar work to the value of Rs. 2,000. The Maharaja of Durbhunga had before him as liberal a scheme of works as he carried out in 1889, but no order had yet been given. This His Honor considered a most laudable record of private liberality at a time when most needed, and he begged to congratulate the different donors on their public-spirited actions.

In the address from the Municipal Commissioners, the remark that a ruler benefited by a knowledge of those he ruled had afforded him pleasure, as it agreed so entirely with his own views, and he was glad to find the District Board has spoken in a very similar sense. His Honor said he did not wish any one to think that tours through different parts of the province were in any way prompted by the least distrust of local officers or fear of being misled by them, but there was such a great advantage in being able to enquire into and discuss local requirements on the spot itself, where far more information could be gained than from any number of written reports.

A reference had been made to the filtered water-supply which this town was fortunate enough to possess, and he congratulated it on being one of the few towns in Bengal which enjoyed such a benefit. He hoped, during his stay, to be able to look into the municipal accounts, to see how the funds were allotted and administered, as mention had been made of the maintenance of the water-works being a heavy charge on their resources. There was to be a new re-assessment of the town, by which it was to be hoped a substantial increase to their funds would be secured. Reference had been made to a promise made by a landholder of the Sonthal-Parganas to present a large sum for the further extension of the water-works, but His Honor said he feared he would be hardly justified in entering into that question, as he knew none of the details and it was not one in which Government could very well interfere. If any gentleman found himself unable to carry out a promise which he had made, Government could hardly compel him to do so; if he had changed his mind in the matter, it was for the Commissioners to use what gentle persuasion they could to lead him back to a better way of thinking. Mention had been made of the long period during which the municipal franchise had been enjoyed in Bhagalpur, and it was satisfactory to find reason to believe that the power had been exercised judiciously and well. The fact of having to reply to addresses on a first arrival at a place, before there had been time or opportunity to become acquainted with it, was unfortunately unavoidable ; but His Honor hoped to be able to see for himself how work had been carried on.

He noticed that in the address a hope had been expressed that Local Self-Government would receive still further expansion in his hands, but His Honor feared that what was really in their minds was to deprecate any restriction rather than to advocate the expansion of Local Self-Government, and that reference was made to the Municipal Amendment Bill which had received some adverse criticism from this point of view. He could, however, assure his hearers that nothing was further from the thoughts or wishes of Government, whose only desire was to take such measures and to make such corrections as would conduce to greater efficiency in the carrying on of the work. Wherever it had occurred to himself or his advisers that flaws existed, they proposed making small modifications in the Act to empower Government to step in, and make small changes without having to use the drastic measures which under the Act were in its power, and the employment of which would bring much discredit to any municipality. It was certainly a much severer measure to abolish a municipality than what was now proposed in the modification in the Bill before Government. He would, however, assure them that the proposed alterations had been circulated for general opinions and remarks, and that all criticism would receive full attention.

The District Board had referred to the heavy drain upon their funds in connection with the famine, and trusted that they would not be called upon to contribute to relief works a larger sum than that which they had set aside for the purpose. He found that they had provided about Rs. 35,000 for these works, being the whole of their balance, and also what would have otherwise been spent on original works. They had also in their budget provided about Rs. 80,000 road repairs, and much of this could be utilised if necessary. His Honor did not think it likely that this provision would be insufficient, but they appeared to have made a very full and excellent distribution. It certainly was not desirable that sums, which were absolutely essential to the good administration of the district, should be diverted to other purposes. The district was well equipped with unmetalled roads, some of them relics of 1874, and it would be a mistake were anything done that would lessen the benefits they conferred. As far as one could foresee, the present distress might continue, or possibly somewhat increase, during the next two months, but with July the rains should come, bringing with them labour in the fields and wages, and in August they might expect to reap their new crops. Should this be so, the present arrangements of the District Board seemed ample. The District Board had rather a tendency to speak of the funds as their own, as if they stood apart from and could even be in opposition to Government; but His Honor said he wished to remind them of the solidarity that should exist between themselves and the Government. He looked on the District Board as almost a Government Department. They were a body of public-spirited gentlemen who gave their voluntary assistance to Government and had public funds placed at their disposal ; but the funds actually belonged to Government, and when they spoke of their proposed allotments, they were in much the same position as Government when framing its budget. He could assure them that the Provincial Government had been cut down by the Provincial contract very severely, and that his position was that he had just enough funds for necessaries but none for luxuries. The Government, like them, had been obliged to withdraw all superfluous grants from other objects to meet the expenses of the present distress, and to cut down many items. It would give him great satisfaction to assist the Board with Provincial funds, or to recoup them their famine expenditure if he could ; but in the present year at least, there was no chance of his having any funds for this purpose.

Referring to the Mahommedan address, His Honor said that he was glad to hear so much had been done for education, and that a Madrassa had been instituted in a manner suited to the requirements of the day in order that Mahommedan boys might not fall behind the rest, and be able to hold their own in competition. Sir Syed Ahmed Khan, in the North-West Provinces, had set them an example which but few could follow closely, but which many now-a-days were striving to follow to some extent ; and every effort made to establish and carry on a system of education for Mahommedans on Mahommedan principles was deserving of Government encouragement. The Mahommedan gentlemen of Bhagalpur were to be congratulated on what they were doing, and would receive such assistance as was fair and just. The request for aid from the Mohsin Fund seemed reasonable, and though the annual fixed sum for grants-in-aid of Buildings had for this year been all allotted, no doubt the Director of Public Instruction would be willing to consider fully their claim when distributing the grants for next year.

His Honor said he had kept till the last a reference to the remark made by the residents of Bhagalpur, when in their address they said : "We venture to express a hope that your Honor will not proceed with the proposed cadastral survey, involving an expenditure on the part of landlords and tenants which they are alike unable to bear." Now, it was not very clear whether this remark was intended to refer exclusively to some possible extension of the cadastral survey to the District of Bhagalpur, or to the work which is actually going on of the survey in North Behar. There was no thought of extending the survey to Bhagalpur at present, but His Honor hoped that so soon as the cadastral survey of Behar had been brought to a successful conclusion, and when the people came to see and understand the enormous advantage that such a complete record of rights conferred upon them, so far from requesting that they might be delivered from it, they would in coming years include in their addresses to his successor a request that the cadastral survey of Bhagalpur might be begun at the earliest possible date. Assuming, however, that the passage related to Behar, and that they were speaking on behalf of their friends and relations in that part of the country, His Honor said he was glad to be able to take advantage of this opportunity to make a few remarks and explanations which he hoped would tend to alay their alarm and anxiety. The objection taken in the address rested on the ground of the expenditure the survey would involve in the present season of scarcity. It was to be hoped however, that the present distress are but a temporary evil. No one could predict the future; but, on the other hand, no one had any valid grounds for anticipating a failure in the coming monsoon; and should all go well, the present trouble would be as completely forgotten next year as the pressure of 1889 was forgotten in 1891. There was every reason to hope that a kind Providence would not afflict the district beyond what it could bear; and that, with the advent of good and seasonable rains, all fears of further scarcity would pass away. So much for the special objection as to the burden of expenditure being aggravated by the present scarcity; but there remained the general objection that the survey would undoubtedly cost money, and he sympathised with their general dislike to have expenditure thrown upon them. In the address, however, mention had been made of the fact that the cost would fall on both landlords and tenants ; but as regarded the latter His Honor did not think there was any need to feel much alarm. As matters stood at the present moment, any ryot who had to defend a rent suit was, sure, first of all, to go to the Collector's cutchery, and there to pay one rupee for a copy of an extract from the Patwari's Jamabandi, which was absolutely of no validity whatsoever, and would not be accepted as evidence in any court. When, however, the proposed survey had been completed, the average ryot would be charged a rupee or thereabouts for a trustworthy and valid statement showing the area, the rent and the number of his fields, and all the incidents of his tenure, and for all this he would pay exactly the same amount as he now had to pay for a document that was perfectly worthless. He was quite sure that any ryots who understood the facts would willingly offer ten times what the survey would cost him, for the sake of the security of the record. He had quite lately had an example of this brought to his notice, in the case of a gentleman in this district, Mr. Hirsch Christian, who holds a ryots tenure in the Baneli-Srinagar Estate, of which a survey and record of rights had lately been carried out by the Court of Wards. That gentleman had informed him that he set the highest value on the record he had secured and that he considered that the survey had been the greatest blessing which could have been conferred upon the estate.

The case of landholders no doubt was somewhat different, and those who owned large tracts of land would have large sums to pay. All that Government could and would do was to try their best to diminish, as far as possible, the disagreeable burden of payment, by spreading it out over a number of years, and to further offer them the assurance that this survey would be to their clear and certain advantage, which, when they had realized and come to understand in its true working, would be accepted by them as even more than an equivalent for any expenditure it might have entailed. His Honor said that his hearers might possibly have noticed the speech he made at the last meeting of the Supreme Legislative Council in Calcutta last month, in connection with the Court of Ward's Bill. He had undertaken there to do all he could to secure for the landlords, in whose estates a cadastral survey had been carried out, a short and summary procedure for the recovery of arrears of rent. When there was no longer any dispute as to whether a man was a tenant or not, and as to what his rent was but only as to how much he had paid and how much was in arrears, he was sure that the summary powers for dealing with such cases which are provided for in the Tenancy Act might fairly be utilised ; and he was in hopes that a shorter procedure, even, might be allowed, corresponding to the power of Government under the Certificate Act.

There was another suggestion for the relief of Zemindars under consideration, concerning which no definite promise could be made beyond the fact that he was favorably disposed towards the scheme of abolishing *patwaris* if it could be done with safety. The suggestion was that there should not be any Government servant retained as accountant in a village, but only the landlord's own accountant, provided security could be given that the accountant, should be competent, and that the landlord would keep up the record of rights in a completely correct condition by entering mutations or other necessary alterations. As it was, his audience knew that at present all alterations in the register of the names and shares of the proprietors were supposed to be carried on by a self-acting system, and there was a penalty prescribed for any omission to register alterations. It was reasonable to think that a similar procedure could be devised for securing the correction of the *Khatians* and *Jamabandis*, and the maintenance of the record of rights from year to year ; and if this were provided, it was quite possible that Government would agree to the abolition of the *patwari*, who is undoubtedly an object of suspicion and dislike to the landlords, and an interminable element of discord.

Although no reference had been made to it in any of the addresses, there was, another point on which he would like to make a few remarks, as he had reason to believe it was one of the chief causes of alarm in connection with the proposed survey specially among the Zemindars, and that was the great expense likely to be incurred on account of the bribes taken and illegal demands that might be made by unscrupulous Amins. It was needless to say that one who had been so long in this country as he himself had been, and had seen so much of the manners and customs of the lower orders of such people, was not prepared to deny the possibility of such demands being made or was ready to undertake the defence of Amins; but though it were impossible to trust to the absolute integrity of these officials, it was both possible and sufficient to rely on the constant supervision and inspection of their work by superior officers with the aid of scientific mathematical instruments. The fears of the malpractices of these Amins were, in fact, due in great part to ignorance of the system to be pursued, and when once the survey was well started and its *modus operandi* understood, it would very easily be seen that such alarm was quite unnecessary. The measures which it was proposed to adopt were that as the Amin went on with his work, measuring and recording in his record, say, about thirty members a day, he should give to the holder of each field a "parcha" or slip showing exactly what had been recorded. This the ryot would take away with him and discuss at his leisure, and at once see whether there was any mistake in the record. During this work it would be quite unnecessary for the Zemindar to detail any person to keep a special watch over the Amins. Everything recorded would thus be brought to light, and its accuracy would be challenged and tested at once; so where would be the use of

an Amin making any false entry ?   When this work had been
completed for a block of villages, the attestation-officer would
come round, who would be either a covenanted officer, such as
an Assistant or Joint-Magistrate or else a Deputy Collector.
He would fix a certain day for the attestation of the khatian,
and have up all the villagers before him, and read out the
record which concerned each in turn, enquiring before all
the assembled crowd if there was any mistake ; and thus the
examination would be easily completed.   At this point only
would it be necessary for the Zemindar to have some trustworthy agent present, able to offer any necessary explanations to the attesting officer, or to assist in settling errors
and disputes, and to protect the Zemindar's interests.   He
hoped that those present, who were connected with Behar,
would explain this method of procedure to their friends, and
that they would see how impossible it would be for an Amin to
make false entries undetected, and how useless for any one to
offer him bribes and to submit to any illegal demands on his part.

He trusted what he had said to-day would be of some
efficacy, both as removing the alarm felt by Zemindars about
the results of the unknown operations of the survey, and also
as disclosing to them what had to be set on the other side of
the account, as advantages which would. accrue to them in
consequence of the survey.   He would further observe that a
conference had lately been held at Muzaffarpur, at which the
Director of Surveys, Colonel Sandeman, and the Commissioner, Mr. Lyall, had met a large number of Zemindars and
Indigo-planters ; and though he had not received an official
report of the proceedings, he had reason to believe that the
explanations offered had been favorably received and had
done much good.   In any case he was sure that in Colonel
Sandeman they would find an officer of great experience and
skill, and one who was most anxious to make the survey go
smoothly, and to meet all reasonable wishes of the parties
concerned.

REPLY TO ADDRESSES FROM THE PEOPLE OF GAYA, OCT., 1892.

His Honor, replying to both these addresses, said that he thanked the members of the Municipal Committee of Gaya, and of the District Board, and the gentlemen representing the residents of the town, very sincerely for the excellent sentiments which animated the addresses just read to him. He cordially reciprocated the feelings expressed in the municipal address, that visits like this must benefit both the people and the Government by making them better acquainted with each other and establishing loyal and friendly regard. From visits of this kind a great and decided advantage was to be gained, for they tended to increase his interest in their wants, and he felt growing in his mind the value of an acquaintance with those with whom he had never before been brought into close contact. He had heard with great pleasure the assurance that the municipality had cleared away the load of debt by which they had so long been hampered in their efforts in the cause of improvement; and now that they would have a surplus at their disposal, he trusted that the time had come when they would be able to take in hand many useful works, and that they would be in a position to carry out their intentions of supplying the town with wholesome fresh water. He was glad to find that they had determined to do so, because the question of supplying the inhabitants with pure water was of the highest importance, and he trusted that the scheme which was being drawn up by one of his ablest Engineers would be a good one, and at the same time not too expensive. He would try to assist them by granting them a loan to enable them to carry out the work, and the interest would in that case be much less than if they obtained the money from any other source. There was one point to which His Honor wished to draw special attention, and it was that when, during the Viceroyalty of Lord Ripon, municipalities were relieved of the charges for maintaining the police, it was distinctly laid down, as part of the contract that the sums thus released should be devoted to the cause of education and to sanitary reforms for the public good. Now at Gaya this contract had been quite ignored, and the reason invariably set forth was the want of funds and indebtedness of the municipality. This excuse no longer existed, and His Honor trusted that in future they would see their way to spending more money on that most important object, and they would fulfil the direct contract which they had made. He would draw their special attention to the importance of primary education in the town. He had some figures here that would astonish them. The boys of a school-going age here amounted to six thousand, but the number of children at present in their schools was only one thousand boys and twenty girls. This fell very considerably below what he expected of them. If they wished to stand their ground in the race, they would do well to remember the great advance Bengal was making in its desire for education. It was not desirable that their girls and boys, their boys especially, should be allowed to grow up in darkness and ignorance. The sum that the municipality had expended on education was only two hundred and seventy-nine rupees, and this was even less than they had expended the year before. He sincerely trusted that the next time he received their municipal report they would have remedied this defect, and that he would find better provision had been made for primary education.

With regard to medical treatment Gaya stood very well, and especially so with regard to the treatment of female patients. They had done an excellent thing in creating a female ward, for the control of which the Dufferin Fund had placed at their disposal a lady doctor, who was, he trusted, acceptable to the ladies of their households, and under whose care he had no doubt it would become more and more useful. He was very glad to hear that funds had been collected for building a female hospital to enable ladies of good families

to enjoy the benefits of medical treatment in seclusion and
primacy, without which their hereditary customs and prejudices would make them shrink from any such institution.

The Municipality in their address had lightly touched
upon the main subject of the address of the Reconciliation
Committee—he meant the melancholy and regretable cir-
cumstance which the recent riot sprang up. He was extremely glad to find that it was not a premeditated affair, and that
it did not occur with the knowledge of the leaders of society
in their town, but that it was owing to the passions of the
lower classes. They were fully aware—and he hardly needed
to impress upon them—that a blow would have been struck
to the prosperity of Gaya and the whole province, if that
riot had been allowed to continue, and that possibly their
streets would have been bathed in the blood of their fellow
citizens. He was extremely glad to find that the riot was
nipped in the bud by the wisdom and prudence of the leading men among them. This was just what one should expect
from them, and it was the heart and soul of the great principle of Local Self-Government which Lord Ripon had done
so much for, and which had taken such a firm root in the
country. It had no more valuable and no more real development than that which was shown when the leading men of the
place came to the front and took the position which their
social standing, wealth, and their education justified them in
taking, and put down any attempt, on the part of the lower
classes to create a disturbance. He, as head of the province
and as representative of the Government, congratulated them
in having among them such men as rose up on this occasion
and he offered his thanks to the gentlemen who distinguished
themselves. There were many who, he understood, assisted
the magistrate on this occasion, but he wished to give special
attention to the names of Moulvi Syed Mahomed Abu Saleh, Mr.
Abdul Halim and Mirza Dost Mahomed as representatives of
the Mahomedan community, Among the Hindu gentlemen he

wished especially to thank on the part of Government the Raja of Maksudpor, Babu Ramanugreh Narayan Singh, the Deputy Magistrate, Babu Ambica Prasad, Rai Rainarayan Singh, Baijnath Singh, Babu Chota Lal Sijwar, and Babu Haldeo Lal.

These gentlemen, he understood, had done no little service to the Government and the town. He thanked them on the part of Government, and he trusted that the people of Gaya would thank them on the part of the town for preserving them from that stain which would have been hard to wipe away and he also trusted that the feeling of reconciliation which they expressed before him was a true and a general one. He had received petitions from a small party of foolish and discontented people asserting that the reconciliation was unreal, but this he refused to believe. These petitions of a few malcontents did not carry any weight with him, and he did not intend to take any notice of them, but to treat them as they deserved to be treated. He accepted the tribute they intended to pay to Mr. Grierson, and he on behalf of the Government wished also to thank him for the wisdom and temperate manner in which he had quelled the discord. He had also heard that Messrs. Lang and Pritchard had given material assistance. As they were young officers, his hearers would closely watch their future career, and if they rose to positions of eminence, the gentlemen here assembled would be able to say that these young men had received their first lesson in Government among them in Gaya. With regard to the well which they wished to sink in recognition of Mr. Grierson's conduct on this occasion, and to call by his name, he was glad to grant them permission to do so, and sincerely trusted that the water of this well would be used to wash away all unkindly feelings among themselves.

REPLY TO ADDRESSES AT DINAJPORE, APRIL, 1892.

His Honor thanked those present sincerely for the very kind and hearty addresses with which they had been good

enough to greet him on this the occasion of his first visit to
the town of Dinajpur, and he fully reciprocated the wishes
expressed by them that the visit might leave nothing but plea-
surable recollections. Certainly the general effect of bringing
a ruler and those under his care into closer association tended
towards better mutual understanding, and to a more hearty
co-operation in matters which they equally had at heart;
and he hoped that, although the present visit was to be of
necessity but a short one it would none the less have this
desirable effect. The chief question touched on in the address
presented by the zemindars was that of the scarcity which
unfortunately prevailed in some parts of the district, and His
Honor said he was glad to be assured that the measures which
had been taken to cope with it were considered to be both
sufficient and effective. The district was very fortunate in
having for its Magistrate, an officer who, though not recently
appointed, had been in Dinajpur in former times, and was
therefore acquainted with the locality and its requirements.
It was a most difficult matter in times like the present to be
able to calculate how far scarcity pressed upon the poorer
people and taxed their resources. With his accurate knowledge of the district in other and more prosperous times, Mr.
Tute was able to contrast the normal state of things with what
he now saw, and was, therefore, able to form a correct judgment as to its present condition and requirements. In the
Commissioner too, the district was fortunate in possessing
an officer who had long served under the Government, and
had for years been the Secretary in that department in which
the management of famine operations lay, and who, therefore,
was thoroughly conversant with the principles which under-
lie the famine Code and with the views and intentions of both
the local Government and the Government of India. It was
satisfactory to learn that what was being and would be done
sufficed to meet any distress there was among those people
who lived chiefly by labouring on the lands, but who, owing to

the failure of the rains and consequent scarcity, had not been able to get the labour that was usually in demand by zemindars and landholders generally, and who, in consequence, had been obliged to seek employment on such works as Government had opened in order to obtain the wherewithal to supply their daily food. The numbers shown in the returns as being on relief works was rather large, but Mr. Tute had explained that many of the works on which the people were employed were not relief works in the proper sense of the word, but were works which the District Board would, under any circumstances, have carried out, and had so arranged as to meet the present demand for work and to a certain extent to derive benefit to themselves by getting their works carried out at a comparatively cheap rate.

This led him to the remark in the address from the District Board about the difficulty that had been experienced in apportioning the sums that were available to the sums that were required for different works. They mentioned that the necessity for providing relief had proved a very severe strain on their resources, and might result in injury to their roads and other works. Possibly that might be true, but it had to be remembered that it was the first duty both of Government and of all District Boards who were the agents or hands of Government to consider which of their requirements were the most pressing, and to allot their funds accordingly. Nothing, his Honor said, had been borne more upon him than the great necessity of providing suitable buildings, more especially in Eastern Bengal, for Munsifs and other similar officers of Government, and he had fully intended this year to give one lakh over and above the usual building grant for the purpose. Scarcity, however, had come upon the land and had necessitated the diversion of this money to another still 'more pressing purpose. The District Board were very much in the same position, and had been obliged to divert a certain portion of their funds in order to benefit the class of people requiring labour by providing work upon the roads. This merely meant the postponement of some original works. No doubt it was very disappointing, but it had perhaps one advantage in teaching them the virtue of patience under circumstances beyond their control, and they might very well say to themselves that though they had been unable to carry out their good intentions this year, they would at any rate do so next year.

Both the District Board and Municipal addresses had referred to the construction of a female hospital and to work being in a forward condition, and his Honor said he had just had great pleasure in seeing what had been done, and congratulated them heartily on what they had undertaken, planned, and commenced. He had often started on previous occasions his opinion that the plans on which female hospitals in many places had been constructed were not on a system quite appropriate to the requirements of the customs of this country. In Calcutta and many other places large female wards had been built on the very same principle as those provided for men, and this was contrary to the very essence of the treatment necessary in the case of women, for even though all males might be rigorously excluded from any portion of the buildings, it was repugnant to the feelings of women of the upper and middle classes to be in a large ward where there might be several others at the same time. The plan of the building which was being erected here was excellent and it was greatly to be hoped that the ladies of the place would soon learn to take advantage of the benefits it conferred, for they might be assured that they would have perfect privacy and that there would be nothing that could in any way shock their sense of modesty. Dinajpur was much to be congratulated, on being the first large town in Bengal that had adopted this right principle of construction.

Next as regarded the question of education. The Municipal Commissioners had started in their address that the cos

of erecting a house for their model school, by which he understood that they meant a middle Vernacular School, had been
so great that they had not been able to do much for primary
education. This excuse would be accepted for the past year,
but in future years it was to be hoped that the Commissioners
would awake to the absolute importance of devoting funds
to this most necessary work. Next to the two great requirements of good drinking water and efficient sanitation to
ensure the health of the body, no duty was so incumbent on
a Municipality as to provide sufficient opportunities for primary
education. Here there were some 1,830 boys of a school-
going age, and till very lately there was not one single primary
school supported by the Municipality. This meant that their
boys were being subjected to a very great drawback, and
would be at a great disadvantage when in the great battle of
life they had to compete with boys of other districts who had
not been so unfortunately circumstanced. His Honor hoped
the Commissioner would very soon see their way to altering
this state of affairs. He was glad to see that one pathshala
had recently been started but it would be necessary to start
a good many more before they could consider the town to be
in a satisfactory condition. Luckily primary education was
very cheap, and sufficient provisions for their 1,830 boys could
easily be supplied for less than one thousand rupees, so the
cost of the measure was not really heavy for the resources of
any Municipality who had the least pretensions to managing
their finances well.

His Honor then came to the important question of the
position of the Municipal Committee. In their address they
had mentioned that the past year was the first in which they
had enjoyed the full privileges of local self-government, so
far as that existed in electing their own Chairman and Vice-
Chairman. For the six previous years their Chairman and
Vice-Chairman had been official, but during the past year
both had been non-official. Their Chairman was a noble-

man of the town and a man of great liberality who had done a great deal by his contribution towards local drainage, and who as head of the local society was a most fitting person for the post. The Vice-Chairman was an able but perhaps somewhat too busy pleader of the town. Well, what had the results of these elections been? The Commissioners had in the address spoken with becoming modesty of their doings. They had said : "We regret to see that the Public Auditor has made an unfavourable report of this Municipality. We are sensible of the mistakes pointed out, and have applied for the services of an Auditor to put our accounts straight and to start afresh on a sound basis. We also intend to increase and reform our collecting staff, and have also taken measures to put our assessments on a proper footing under the guidance of our Magistrate." These sentiments were so excellent and so wise that it was difficult to say anything severe of the occurrence which had led to their necessity. He was most unwilling to use such an occasion as this—an occasion of friendly and cordial meeting, when the loyalty to Government which inspired them all found its expression in a cordial address to himself, which gave him sincere pleasure—for uttering any words of censure or reproof, and still more so when they had disarmed him by the cordial confession that they were alive to their own shortcomings. But, still, as a matter of history, for their own instruction as to the lesson to be learned from the past, as well as for the future guidance of other Municipalities in Bengal, it would not be wise to pass over too lightly the errors and failures of the past year's experiment. When local self-government was first instituted in the time of Lord Ripon, it was started with the full consciousness that mistakes would occur, for everyone in the world made mistakes, but it was also started in the belief that the experience which would be gained through these very mistakes would result in producing such experience and political training and knowledge of the art of Government as would more than counterbalance any evil results. The Magistrate, Mr. Tute, had made a most careful inspection of the Municipality and its official records, and in his report had pointed out how the Municipal finance, sanitary conditions, and other matters had not merely fallen into arrears, but had actually gone back. He had pointed out how many sanitary improvements had been actually abolished and insanitation permitted to start afresh; how the Commissioners had decided that private tanks could not be cleaned out without a separate report for each and instructions as to the method of doing it from the Civil Medical Officer.

As these or similar tanks had existed and been cleaned for hundreds of years, surely such advice and instruction as how to do the work were unnecessary. The assessment of the town had been left in a most irregular condition, and the collections had fallen so much into arrear that at the end of the past year there was an uncollected balance of over Rs. 6,000. In the previous year when the Chairman had been a Government official, the total arrears had been some Rs. 1,100 only. Of course it was impossible to prevent having some arrears, owing to deaths, departures, and so forth, but the amount this year had been so large that it was satisfactory to find the Commissioners had recognised the error of their ways, and had resolved to take such steps that in future no such blame could be laid at their doors. Again, they had made an unfortunate mistake as regards the loan for the drainage of the town which had been provided, but which the Commissioners had resolved not to take up. They had recently changed their minds and applied for the loan, and His Honor had been compelled to reply that, as the whole sum provided in the budget for such loans had now been allotted, it was impossible to grant the request in the current year. This misfortune was due to their own procrastination, but it might have the advantage of saving them from the results of procrastination on future occasions. This spirit in which their address had concluded was a very right and proper one, and it was very certain that with the assistance of Mr. Tute they would be able in future to avoid similar mistakes, and would experience but little difficulty in wiping off their arrears.

Reverting to the address of the District Board, His Honor mentioned the request that the Government would forego the interest due on the instalment of Rs. 40,000 for this year of the loan of two lakhs which had been taken up for permanent improvements. This instalment, they said, had been put aside and was not to be utilised for fear of necessity arising for meeting the expense of further relief works. His Honor said he had had no opportunity of consulting the Financial Department, but he was pretty certain that if they had drawn the advance from the Treasury, they could be allowed to refund it, and if it had not already been drawn there was no necessity for taking it this year, and in either case the charge for interest could be remitted. His Honor then concluded by again thanking those present for their friendly welcome, and assuring them how real a pleasure it had been to him to make their acquaintance.

REPLY TO ADDRESSES FROM INHABITANTS OF THE DISTRICT OF PURI.

" I have to thank you for the address of welcome you have just read, and for the kind manner in which you have greeted me on my arrival in this place. I must, however, confess to a feeling of regret that the terms in which I am about to reply are not of the kind one likes to employ on an occasion like the present, when the Municipal Commissioners are assembled to meet their Lieutenant-Governor; when they ordinarily have a report of good work and progress to present ; and when it is the natural result of such a meeting that all should afterwards separate with an increased regard for each other. The present, however, is an occasion on which, while wishing to treat you with the utmost courtesy, I should be failing in my duty, both to Government and to yourselves, were I not to explain in what way you have omitted to carry out your duties, and to point out to your shortcomings. I fully appreciate what you have said as regards the unusual difficulties with which you have to contend, and I admit that it must be often hard to carry out certain works in such a manner as not to offend the religious prejudices or principles of the people whom you represent. It would neither be right for you to offend those prejudices, nor for the Government even to ask you to do so, but there are many matters connected with good administration and sanitation, into which the question of religious prejudice does not in any way enter, and I would invite you to take much more active steps in these matters than you have hitherto been in the habit of doing. In the first place, you put forward the plea of poverty as an excuse for the present state of affairs, and say that, when the Lodging House Fund raises its contribution from Rs. 4,000 to Rs. 6,coo, supplemented by a possible grant of Rs. 2,000 from the District Board you hope to be able to carry out great improvements; but I wish to draw your particular attention to the amount of income which is already yours, and which you do not even take the trouble to collect. During the three-quarters which have elapsed of the year 1891, the demand on account of latrine-tax, house-tax and land-rent amounted to the sum of Rs. 28,000, but you only collected Rs. 14,500, or very little over half the amount due to you. Now what is the use of your talking of the works you are going to do with an increased grant of Rs. 4,000 from other sources when you do not take the trouble to collect Rs. 13,500 of the funds to which you are already entitled? These remarks refer to the income which you are entitled to collect. But that income ought to be increased. The present assessment of the town was settled in 1888, and in the year 1891 the time came round for a new assessment, when, very correctly, you divided up the town into different portions, and allotted one to every two

Commissioners, telling them to draw out lists of houses and to visit and assess them according to their true value. But having done this you did no more; the work was never carried out, and I am told that up to the present day not one single Commissioner has ever given in his record of re-assessment."

"Regarding the expenditure of the funds you have actually received, I do not feel called on to make very unfavorable remarks on the manner of its distribution. On education, however, I find you spend almost nothing; nothing is done for vaccination, and for registration but very little, your funds are limited, it is true, and I admit that the conservancy and cleaning of the roads necessitated by the great traffic caused by pilgrimages require an unusually large part of your available means; but it is necessary to point out to you how serious the results of these limitations are. You have hitherto only afforded a little aid to one Middle Vernacular School and one Girls' School, and you have recently promised the Magistrate to open some Primary Schools. What I would urge upon you is, that sufficient opportunities for primary education should be afforded for all boys of a school-going age, to enable them to receive sufficient education to hold their own in competition with the boys of other parts of Bengal. It seems to be a freely admitted fact among you all, that Orissa is very backward in the matter of education, and yet you have hitherto done almost nothing towards affording your boys improved facilities for acquiring education. Personally I should be very glad to find every office in Orissa filled with Urya officials, and I am sure that Mr. Toynbee, the Commissioner, agrees with me; but of course, Government are bound to accept the best candidate they can get. If a Bengali and an Urya candidate of nearly equal qualifications come forward, there is no doubt, but that the latter will be taken ; but if the Bengali shows decided superiority, then, of course, Government is bound to accept him. I wish you, therefore, to very seriously consider this question of providing larger means of education."

"I have been speaking so far of the amount of money which you have spent; but now I would like just to look into the question whether it is well and judiciously spent. About 48 per cent. of your funds have been laid out on conservancy and road cleaning; but has all that might have been done with this money been actually done? Going through your town yesterday and to-day, I have found that most houses have cesspools which open on and discharge into the street. Such a filthy state of things I have seen in no other town in Bengal, and it is very certain there can be no possible offence to religious principles in altering this. The conservancy arrangements are at present of the poorest and most offensive type and the cesspools could be easily arranged to discharge their contents into reservoirs at the back of the houses instead of on to the street front. Most of your houses seem to be well and strongly built, standing on well-raised stone plinths, and you have therefore every element for a good drainage system, and yet the present state of things exists. The cost of these charges ought not to fall upon the Municipality, but they should be carried out at the expense of the owners of the houses. Then, again, the state of the public burial-ground for paupers has been described as horrible. Your Magistrate Mr. Allen, very rightly recommended you to build a burning place, and you erected a good *Chabutra* (platform) with surrounding walls for cremation; but as soon as the Magistrate went away on leave and turned his back, you turned yours also, and permitted the *Chabutra* to fall into disuse and disrepair. Now this sort of conduct is neither creditable to you nor to that system of local self-Government which has, perhaps, the reputation of being more flourishing and better appreciated in Bengal than in any other part of India. The next question is that of the four great sacred tanks in the town. Some of them are very fine, but at the same time the water in them must be very unwholesome, and there can be very little doubt but that they are a great source of disease among the large number of pilgrims who come to them. It is very certain that something must be done to cleanse these large sacred tanks. The tank, which is the most sacred of all, called the Setgunga tank, is in the very midst of your houses, and as it is very deep and the water level is very low, it is therefore very foul, indeed; and yet the Municipal Commissioners do not seem even to have thought out any plan for cleaning it. Recently, during a visit to Gya, I came across just such another deep and foul tank surrounded by houses, but when it was pointed out to him, the Mohant at once promised to have it dewatered and cleaned out, and made no difficulty about the matter. Surely what was possible in Gya must be equally so here. It would be very gratifying, therefore, to hear that some wealthy Mohant or other gentleman had come forward and undertaken to do the work. If, however, this should not happen, the Municipality must do it themselves, and if they raise objections to the work, then Government must enforce it. It seems to me that the best and only method of cleansing and keeping the tank clean will be to put in some sort of pucca flooring, and to repair the masonary sides, so as to prevent any drainage entering the tank, and to have the water changed at least once a year."

"And, now, gentlemen, having drawn your attention to these matters, I must tell you that I have been very seriously considering what steps it will be necessary for the Government to take. The one course open under the present Municipal Act is to issue an order, under section 64, and if it is not obeyed, then under Sections 65 and 66 to suspend the Municipality; but this would have entailed great discredit on all concerned, and undoubtedly the vernacular papers would have taken up the subject and pointed at Puri the finger of scorn. But another course will very shortly be opened, for in an amended Municipal Bill, which is now being considered, there is a proposal that Government should have power to put a Municipality into Schedule 2. There are already some municipalities under this schedule, but by some unfortunate oversight such a rule as is now being proposed was omitted in the original Act. I am anxious specially to draw your attention to this amending Bill, because I see that an agitation is being got up against it and people are saying that I am aiming a blow at Local Self-Government, and instituting a retrograde measure. This is a complete mistake, and the working of the Municipal law in Puri is a good example of the benefit which my proposed amendment will do. Instead of passing an order which will convey a direct and severe censure, a milder policy will be opened. When this amendment has been passed, Government will have the power to order any Municipality to be placed in the second schedule, and will then be able to order the Chairman to be a Government official, and to see that work is properly carried out. It would, however, be pleasanter and more satisfactory if you yourselves were to move in this direction, and ask your present Chairman to resign, and take care to appoint in his place an official who is trained in sanitary matters, and is strong enough not only to give the necessary orders, but to see also that they are efficiently carried out. Such an official will be found in your Civil Surgeon, who is naturally designated as the most suitable Chairman of such a municipality as this. I have no present intention of putting the power vested in Government under the old Act into operation by suspending the Municipality, but as soon as the new Act has been passed, I mean to appoint an official Chairman. If you choose to do so, you have the power to forestall my intention in the manner I have just suggested.

"Before closing this reply I wish to refer to another subject. There is sitting in Calcutta at the present time a voluntary Committee to take measures on behalf of the sanitation of Puri, and the town owes a great debt of gratitude to its members and especially to Babu Jadu Lal Mullick, and

Babu Raj Kumar Sarbadhikari, the Secretary, for all the trouble
they have taken for the improvement of this place. I think,
however, the Committee are somewhat mistaken in attributing
to the water supply the cause of so much illness and suffering
among the pilgrims. There is no dearth of wells containing
good water in the town from which the residents obtain their
supplies, and from which pilgrims also could get theirs, and
if the residents do not suffer from the water, it cannot surely
be said that the well water is the cause of disease among the
pilgrims. There must, therefore, be some special cause affect-
ing the pilgrims alone, as the Magistrate, Mr. Allen, has
very justly remarked, and this cause no doubt is the insanitary
habits of the pilgrims, and their custom of drinking the
polluted-water of the sacred tanks in which diseased people
bathe as freely as any other. No doubt, too, many of the
pilgrims arrive from long distances, feeble and exhausted,
and therefore more susceptible to disease. Mr. Allen has in
a praiseworthy manner been devoting himself to the general
welfare of these travellers before they reach Puri, and has
been endeavouring to lessen the hardships of the road by
establishing and improving chatties, by erecting hospitals,
and appointing health-officers and special native doctors at
the season the pilgrims are most numerous. The other probable cause of disease remains, and it is my intention to have
a proper analysis made of the water in each of these large
tanks, and also of the water from three or four of the most
used wells. If the well water is found, as we believe, to
be good, then the question must be considered as to whether there are sufficient wells, and if not, then more must be
constructed. If the tank water is as bad as I conceive, every
nerve must be strained to purify it, and keep it clean, and in
these combined ways, by looking after the health of the pilgrims on the road to and from Puri, by protecting and
increasing the supply of well-water, and by turning the tank
from receptacles of liquid sewage to reservoirs of fair whole-

some water, I trust we may succeed in lessening the terrible mortality among the unfortunate pilgrims, and effacing the stigma which now attaches to this place."

SPEECH IN THE VICEROY'S COUNCIL ON THE COURT OF WARDS' AMENDMENT BILL.

His Honor the Lieutenant-Governor of Bengal spoke as follows:—What had been said by the two Hon. Members who preceded him, Mr. Evans and Sir Phillip Hutchins, as to two of the main subjects under discussion, *viz.*, as to the power of the Court of Wards to intervene in the management of undivided shares in estates, and as to the general principle of allowing a proprietor to declare himself disqualified to manage his estate, had been so fully stated and so entirely accorded with his own views, that it was unnecessary for him to say anything more on those subjects. His Honor turned therefore to the third main subject of the day, the applicability of the certificate procedure to Wards' Estates, and would proceed with great pleasure to answer the challenge which had been thrown down by the Hon. Mr. Evans, who had practically asked from the head of the local Government a pledge that an executive order should issue preventing the use of the certificate procedure in a certain class of cases, and that the earliest possible opportunity should be taken to amend the Certificate Act in the same direction. His Honor answered that he gave that pledge with pleasure, and readily undertook to do what the High Court and the Hon. Member desired should be done. He fully agreed with what had been said by Mr. Evans as to the condition of things which generally was found to exist, when the Court of Wards first took over an estate of a deceased proprietor. They generally found that the estate was in a condition of great confusion, and the accounts and rent-roll were incorrect and untrustworthy. It was not a fair thing then for the ryot that the manager of an estate under the Court of Wards should have legal power given to him to act upon the rent-roll and the lists of arrears and other papers as if they were thoroughly proved and reliable, and to issue certificates and take out execution for rents due, and leave the onus of proof, that the rent was not due, upon the ryot. But while admitting that this was not the right position in which to place the ryot, he did not believe that the law had often or usually been worked so as to cause real injustice, and he was glad that the Hon. Mr. Evans had guarded himself from making a charge against the officers of Government, and had protected those officers from having a charge made against them which would have had no foundation. The Hon. Member very justly said that although the legal position of the ryot was an improper one, there was no doubt that the Managers of estates did their best to do justice, in spite of the temptation to show clean rent-sheets and a full collection of rents. The Rent Courts before which these requisitions came would, as a rule, be quite as careful to ensure that the decree was not made against the ryot upon insufficient grounds as a Civil Court would. His Honor thought his hon. friend had in some slight degree exaggerated the idea that the Managers of Wards' Estates were consumed with a desire to show their zeal and efficiency by a punctual collection of rents. It had been his duty to study and to review the annual report in which the Board of Revenue set forth the demands and collections in the Wards' Estates; and, as a matter of fact, that report showed that heavy arrears existed in many estates, and that it was a rare thing for the entire demand of the year to be collected within the year. If on any future occasion he should be inclined to attribute these arrears to laxity or neglect he would bear in mind his honorable friend's theory that the large balances are due, not to want of zeal, but to assiduous care, to do justice, and he would abstain from censure accordingly. But leaving this point and returning to the main question, His Honor desired to state, in as clear language as was possible, what he intended to do to carry out the pledge

4

now given. He fully agreed that a summary procedure for unrecovery of rent was not a suitable process in any case where a dispute existed as to what the amount of the rent really was; and the order which he proposed to issue was that as soon as an Estate came under the Court of Wards, the first duty of the Court would be to carry out the provisions of Section 101 and the following Sections of the Bengal Tenancy Act, to make a settlement between landlord and tenant, including a field survey and the completion of the record of rights: and till the record of rights was made, and every dispute between landlord and ryot was definitely settled, he was of opinion that the certificate, or any form of summary procedure, was not justified. His Honor further undertook that he would take the earliest possible steps in conjunction with his legal advisers to carry out the amendment of the law so as to make the procedure under the Certificate Act agree with what he would prescribe by executive Resolution.

His Honor thought that the Hon. Member Mr. Evans had been very well advised in not pushing his objections to the certificate procedure to the extent of trying to bar the passing of this Bill or inserting provisions restricting the application of the Certificate Act in the case of the few estates which would be newly brought by this Bill under the Court of Wards. By the course he had taken he had ensured the extension of the revised procedure not only to the new estates, but to all those already under the Court or falling under the old law. But there was a still wider vista which might be opened out to them in connection with this matter. It was one which he thought was of considerable importance and he was glad of this opportunity of laying it before the Council. He came down to this Council having no doubt about the proposal which he was about to make: but, since he had been there, some slight doubt had crept into his mind, after what had fallen from the Legal Member. Sir Alexander Miller had expressed his opinion that a summary procedure might be suitable for the recovery of the Government demand of revenue but could in no way be suitable in the adjustment of a dispute between landlord and tenant. His Honor trusted when the Legal Member had an opportunity of seeing the great accuracy with which the record of rights under the Tenancy Act was made, and how distinctly every incident of the tenure was defined, and what care was taken to settle all disputes and record all the facts of the case, when the Hon. Member had satisfied himself on the subject, he would agree that a summary procedure might be allowed as safely for the recovery of rent as for the recovery of Government revenue. The Council were aware that the local Government were engaged not merely in the Cadastral Survey of these estates, as to which His Honor had pledged himself, but also in surveying a large portion of these provinces, and these operations had given rise to great anxiety on the part of many landholders and ryots. His Honor thought it would be some satisfaction to them, and some alleviation of their anxiety, if they could be assured that, as soon as these records of rights, which would be formed under the Bengal Tenancy Act, had been drawn up, some summary procedure, like that for the recovery of rents by Government, would be adopted and that landlords would practically obtain the same benefits in regard to the recovery of their rents as Government officers now had in regard to the recovery of rents in the estates which belonged to Government, and those which are under the management of the Court of Wards. There was a provision in the Tenancy Act under which rent suits below Rs. 50 may be tried summarily like Small Cause Court suits, but this provision had not been put in force hitherto, because rent suits generally have turned, not on the mere question whether the rent has been paid or not, but on the question how much the rent properly is, or whether rent is due at all. When once disputes of this sort had been cleared away, it seemed probable that the provision referred to might be utilised, or even that some simpler procedure might be invented.

His Honor promised that this subject should be taken in hand by the Bengal Government at the earliest opportunity, and he trusted that, with the sanction of the Government of India, he would be able to carry out measures or possibly to introduce a Bill of this kind which would extend the benefits to all classes and would do a great deal to remove the disputes and anxieties now arising between landlord and tenants, as well as to allay the opposition to the Cadastral Survey.

INDEX.

5